WHAT THE BODY REQUIRES

a symphonic novel

Also by Debra Di Blasi

Fiction
Ugly Town: the movie
The Jirí Chronicles and Other Fictions
Prayers of an Accidental Nature
Drought & Say What You Like

Nonfiction
Seize Your Diem: The Guide to Creative WordPlay

WHAT THE BODY REQUIRES

a symphonic novel

Debra Di Blasi

Jaded Ibis Press
an imprint of Jaded Ibis Productions, Inc.
Kansas City, Missouri U.S.A.

Debra Di Blasi

COPYRIGHTED MATERIAL

Cover design and illustrations by Debra Di Blasi. Illustrations
are adapted from Michelangelo's *Creation of Adam,
Creation of Eve, Judgment Day,* and *The Expulsion,* in the
Sistine Chapel.

"Singing music to a saddened soul is like
dropping vinegar upon a wound."

—Proverbs 25:20

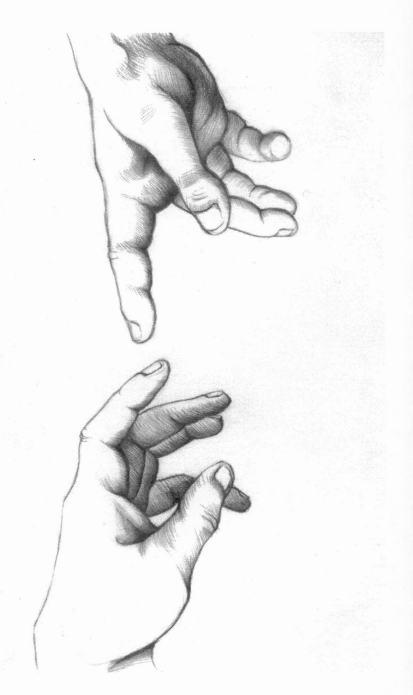

I. Prelude
Another sun, another life

Massimo Benevento kneels in his ill-fitting police uniform upon the straw beside the dead goat and peers into its eye. Gold eye like the sun setting over the sea of another country where it is warm always and without such troubles, big or small. He knows this is an ordinary goat, an ordinary death. Yesterday it was the ordinary death of chickens. The day before, an ordinary infant stillborn. The day before that, an ordinary old man without legs. It is a cold winter and ordinary death occurs inside it. There will be more deaths before it is over. This he knows, too.

He pries open the goat's mouth and looks down its throat. He taps its hollow ribcage, examines a cloven hoof. He strokes the chilled hide of its belly and sighs, "Ah, *sí, sí, sí!*" He stands, brushes the straw from the knees of his police uniform, takes out a small notebook and writes in Italian:

> It is a goat. A dead goat. Its eyes are gold like the sun. Not the sun of Bagno di Tristezza, not the sun of Italy. Another sun. In another country.
>
> Must one die to have a new life?

Debra Di Blasi

II. Adagio
¿Que es una vida sin musica?

— one —

What is a life without music? The old woman picking
olives from the gnarled trees along Via Veleno would
say death. It's the first of December and the olives
have been ripe for a week. She stands on a wooden
ladder, her round body heaving against her thin cotton
dress. While she picks she hums tunes from old
American movies. It's the first of December and forty
degrees Fahrenheit. She hums and her breath weaves
through the silver branches. She wears no gloves, is
perhaps no more than sixty, but her hands would tell
you ninety. They are as swollen and twisted as the
trees she cleans of black fruit. There is a rag tied to her
waist because sometimes her fingers bleed. The grove
is not even half picked and already the rag is stained by
her bleeding fingers.

But she is humming. Today it's Moon River.

Each morning Madeline Rivera walks by and calls
out, "Giorno!"

The woman nods and keeps humming. It's forty
degrees and she sweats in her thin cotton dress and
hums. Ask her: What is a life without music? If she
stops humming long enough to answer she will say,
Death.

Dear Gustavo: One of these mornings when she is humming a tune I'm particularly fond of, I will stop and listen. I will smoke a cigarette and look out across this valley of crumbling villas and olive groves and cold mud roads and will listen to her hum and feel the blood surge from my head to my clitoris and curl my toes inside these black black shoes and come screaming all of the pigeons to flight. I won't be cheating. I'll still be within the boundaries of the game. Accidental music, music that occurs spontaneously, music encountered by chance, music that is not music... These are acceptable because they must be. If I dream I am singing Aida it's not my fault.

— two —

The owner of the dead goat stands on tiptoe, trying to peer over Massimo's shoulders. Massimo smiles to himself, raises the notebook higher and writes in Italian, in block letters large enough for the man to read:

DEAD GOAT. ACCIDENT? OR <u>MURDER</u>?

The old man gasps, *"Mio dios!"* and throws a withered hand over his chest.

Massimo chuckles to himself, slaps shut the notebook, and steps outside into the rain. Below is another villa, its garden full of weeds and brambles and saplings. He takes the binoculars from his car and peers through them far below at the woman in the black coat and scarf. He watches her light a cigarette, walk toward him, gaze with gray eyes that see through his uniform into a heart that races with imagination toward a future tucked behind the emptiness of her gray eyes.

The villa owner drags the dead goat out of the stable to the dry lee under the eaves. "The season is bad, Lieutenant Benevento," he warns. "An evil season."

Massimo reluctantly lowers his binoculars. He turns to watch the old man douse the goat with kerosene and set it afire.

– three –

It is exactly one and a half kilometers from the villa to the post office. How does Madeline know this? Stefano told her and she believes him.

Stefano owns the villa, lives on the first floor with his blind wife, Angelina, and sick dog, Topi. He mournfully confesses that when he's drunk he trips Angelina and kicks Topi, so why should he lie about kilometers?

December 1.

Three weeks Madeline has made this walk to and from *la posta*. Three weeks to the day. Twenty-one days. Sixty-three kilometers. She knows this road by its music:

Here is Topi, waiting for her just outside the heavy wooden gate of the garden. It's 8:30. After three weeks Topi knows exactly when Madeline will lift the rotting latch. The gate creaks shut behind her, and here is Topi – wheezing, wagging her tail, quivering with anticipation and disease. Stefano kicks Topi when he's drunk. What Topi knows of Madeline is a hand passing gently over her bony spine.

Stefano blames Madeline for Topi's longevity. He says that before Madeline came to the villa Topi lay in the wood shed choking on her own blood, waiting for death to come and free her of pain. "But *you* come," Stefano tells Madeline in broken English. "You come and Topi have – *speranza*."

"Hope?"

"*Sí*, yes, hope."

Last winter in another country, a lifetime ago, someone abandoned a lame pup in the alley behind Madeline's studio. That area of the city filled with warehouses and failing businesses was vacant except for Madeline and a few other artists who had set up studios there, paying minimal rents and working through the odd, silent hours of night. Madeline listened to Wagner's *Tristan Und Isolde*. She listened because she did not love Wagner's music and was painting violent abstractions eight feet high and five feet wide and black and red and gray. Her *Balkan Series*. Wagner, of course, was German, but it didn't matter. Her distaste for his music fueled her anger over the atrocities in Eastern Europe – rape and land mines, torture and mass graves – anger heavy as grief heavy as Wagner and so she thought she'd be safe.

But the music caused the walls to tremble and the fine hairs on the back of Madeline's neck to bristle. She turned up the stereo full volume, and her pulse quickened and the black paint went on thicker and the red sliced through the black and she was angry, angry, angry and aroused by her anger – a force that propelled her from painting to painting, orgasm to orgasm, day to day. As the music swelled toward climax so did her cunt, and she only had to gently stroke the crotch of her jeans to bring herself to orgasm. Which she did. Gripping, always, a broad brush thick with red paint that she slid over the canvas while she came and Wagner's horned soprano screamed.

During the night a shrill wailing like a discordant horn entered the music. Madeline thought it was Wagner and so kept painting. But the wailing continued beyond the music, filled the alley completely and bled through the wide windows of the studio.

She took the service elevator down to the loading dock and stepped out into the alley. A pup had been stuffed into a burlap sack and then tossed into dumpster. The wailing stopped the moment Madeline lifted the dumpster's lid. She dug through a foot of trash before she found the pup – a black Labrador, no more than three months old. One of its hind legs had atrophied, was a third shorter than the others, and hung like a broken tree branch, swaying with each step.

Madeline set the pup down on the cold greasy pavement. It stood mute and expectant. She shoved her hands into her coat pockets and stared at it. It stared at Madeline and shivered.

From a high window a chorus sang recriminations.

"Wagner," Madeline snorted.

The pup sprang to life, whipping its tail so violently back and forth that its entire body twisted in one long continuous spasm.

"Wagner," she repeated, louder.

The pup gave a single yap and tried to climb up Madeline's pant leg, tumbling over backward when its one good hind leg gave out.

Madeline gathered the pup in her arms and took it home.

She had Wagner, the pup, one week before Gustavo found out about it.

Gustavo had gone snow camping with his good friend Bernard Allande. At least that's what Gustavo told Madeline. He said, "Madeline, I'm going snow camping with my good friend Bernard Allande." For two weeks Gustavo allegedly camped in the snow with his good friend Bernard Allande. For one week Wagner kept Madeline company.

She took him to the studio and told him about the former Yugoslavia's woes while she painted and Wagner chewed on one of Gustavo's old loafers. Until then, so much of her time away from Gustavo had been spent in solitude, painting inside the pulse of this music or that: soundtracks for anger and masturbation. Often she'd felt the solitude driving her mad. Wagner's company, though voiceless, was a reprieve.

Then Gustavo returned from his alleged camping trip with chapped lips and a sour mood. He took one look at Wagner and said no.

Madeline frowned. "What do you mean, *no?*"

"No dog."

"Why not?"

"Dogs are not allowed in the apartment, Maddi. You know this."

"We'll move."

Gustavo clucked his tongue and shook his head and walked into the bathroom.

"I want him!" Madeline shouted.

"You don't need him! You have me!"

The toilet flushed.

Dear Gustavo: They killed Wagner. They gave him an injection and he went to sleep and did not wake up again. Wagner made me happy.

Gustavo smiled, "But, Maddi, you still have me."

Dear Gustavo: Wagner is dead in Missouri. I'm alive in Italy. Where the hell are you?

Madeline slides two fingers from the end of Topi's dry nose to her balding head. White hair comes loose and floats away in the wind. Topi squints, blinking rapidly, and moans. Mucous rattles in her throat. The dog will follow Madeline for one hundred meters. No further. For one hundred meters the road curves downward, then slopes sharply upward. It's a difficult climb for even Madeline, who's thirty-two and as healthy as these oaks. Topi is old and sick and knows the limits of her body.

Madeline walks.

Topi gazes after her, then shifts her gaze as the wind shifts, bringing down from the distant hills the scent of Massimo who peers through binoculars at Madeline and thinks of salt – salt of a woman, salt of the sea – and of a place inside both. He lowers the binoculars. Sighs, "Ah, *sí, sí, sí.*" Feels the pleasant pressure of his cock against his trousers. Watches. Strokes the rough black fabric over his zipper. Imagines Madeline's white hips and pink nipples. Trembles in a uniform too tight in the cold-sharpened wind.

Perpetual wind hissing through dry grass and fallen leaves. It does not stop in this valley. In summer it comes all the way from the African coast to cross this foreign landscape. The cypress and oaks and pines on the surrounding hills shudder and sway always. But it's winter now. The first of December. The African wind has surrendered to the hard chill blowing down from the north, and the mud of this road is packed solid and cold as marble. Madeline walks and walks on the cold mud road. Her breath is visible, a thin mist that reminds her she's not dead yet.

Here is the clear shallow stream flowing beneath the lowest point of the road. To the right the water drops into a deep gully and cuts through thickets and bedrock on its way to the Arno River. To the right the stream is nothing more than a whisper. But to the left — here is the difference! To the left the water slips over worn gray stones and sounds like wind chimes.

Wind chimes...wind chimes...wind chimes?

No. Not exactly. Precision is everything now. Precisely: To the left the water sounds like a hand passing through the thin prisms of a chandelier.

A chandelier hung in the living room of their apartment in another country, another life. Brass with five tiers of overlapping prisms, forming an inverted pyramid. In the mornings the sun would come through the front windows and strike the prisms and scatter a hundred tiny rainbows over the walls. The rainbows were lovely, but Madeline did not buy the chandelier because of rainbows. She bought it because when she passed a hand through the prisms they would clink against one another and there would be music, and the music made her happy.

She would sit at the window or lie on the bed, sighing, waiting for Gustavo to finish practicing his violin, waiting for Gustavo to fold his fingers around her instead. Then she would grow tired of waiting and walk through the living room and raise a hand and trail her fingers through the thin crystal prisms and there would be music and she'd smile and she'd want Gustavo more.

Gustavo hated the chandelier. He hated it because Madeline always passed a hand through the prisms while he practiced his violin. He said the sound was a distraction and only noise. She said it was music and it made her happy to hear it.

"*Por favor,*" Gustavo would plead, "do not do that again."

And Madeline would stand beneath the chandelier and look at Gustavo and raise a hand and sweep it through the prisms again. "This is music, too," she'd tell him, "and it makes me happy."

Gustavo would sneer. "Shit. What do you know about music?"

Dear Gustavo: I know that when the water of this stream flows over these stones it sounds like a hand passing through the thin prisms of a chandelier. I know this stream is music, too. I know you would also hate the music of this stream. I know that because you would hate it, I love it.

One hundred meters.

Here the road slopes sharply upward. Madeline begins the ascent, then stops and turns. There is Topi standing just beyond the stream, looking at Madeline with wet eyes and quivering.

Madeline waves. "*Ciao,* Topi!"

Topi gives a sudden leap upon hearing her name, then hesitates. She will not climb the hill with Madeline. Instead, she will watch Madeline keep walking until Madeline disappears beyond the old church. Then she will let out one pitiful bark and stand at the bottom of the hill for God knows how long before finally laying her rasping body down in the dry grass along the road where she will sleep until Madeline returns.

Someday Madeline will walk back down this hill and find Topi alongside the road, curled in the dry grass. Madeline will walk softly up to wake Topi, and Topi will be dead. Madeline is certain of this.

Dear Gustavo: Without music, the inevitabilities of life begin shouting.

– four –

Madeline loved beautiful things. She wanted to own them. Gustavo was beautiful.

The opening night of her first major exhibition, a wild dark storm swept through the Midwest, knocking down power lines, tearing branches from trees, shattering windows with hail the size of a child's fist. The gallery stood like a fortress against the storm. Art patrons stumbled through the door with wet coats and torn umbrellas and frowns. The warm dry light of the gallery made them smile, and relax.

But not Madeline's paintings.

A critic studied each one, then studied Madeline. "You are an angry woman," he said. He peered through the gallery windows. "Outside a storm is raging," he said, then turned and tapped Madeline's forehead with a fat, cold finger. "Inside here it's the same."

Madeline said, "Well," and walked away.

In a corner of the gallery a string quartet played Mozart: *String Quartet in G Major, Opus 387*. Gustavo stood dead center, playing his violin. He was serious and beautiful. His long brown fingers beautiful. His black hair beautiful. His lips beautiful.

Mozart.

Madeline had asked for Wagner.

"But you do not like Wagner," said Gustavo.

"Precisely," said Madeline.

"We will play Mozart."

"It's important I have Wagner."

"But you cannot have him."

"Wagner."

"No."

"Please."

"Mozart or *nada.*"

The string quartet played Mozart: *String Quartet in D Minor, Opus 421.* The music drowned the noise of hail on the roof. Madeline stood in the middle of the gallery and watched Gustavo slide his bow over the strings, a delicate persistent gesture. Erotic. His expression erotic, too: eyes half closed, brows arched, lips gaping and wet. Every woman turned from her husband's side to stare at Gustavo. Eventually even the husbands turned to stare.

An old woman with a Slavic accent, her eyes moist with awe, said to no one in particular, "Look at him. He is beautiful!"

"Yes," said Madeline, "and he is mine."

Paris, France
November 21

My delicious Madeline:

I'm enclosing a postcard of Michelangelo's *The Creation of Adam.* (I had to pass through Rome again so I stopped off at the Sistine Chapel.) The postcard doesn't do the original justice, of course. There's something unsettling, almost shocking, about Adam's beauty.

Michelangelo believed the body was the manifestation of the soul, but I think it's the opposite. I think it's the manifestation of what the soul lacks. Beauty like Adam's is oppressive. It's a burden to recognize it, to feel the weight of it. I feel its weight. I've felt it. I had to get out of there, out of the Chapel, it depressed me so much. But maybe it's only because I'm missing you.

After this is over we can go to the Chapel together and look at *The Creation* and maybe it'll inspire me. You inspire me. You're my Eve.

With my deepest love, Cliff

Cliff. Clifford. Clifford Beale.

Whose friend was he first? Gustavo's or Madeline's? Madeline can no longer remember, though she stares down at the cold mud of Via Veleno and tries.

Clifford Beale lived in the apartment next door, in another country, a lifetime ago. He was a graduate student of linguistics, fluent in five languages, and lover of opera. At night he played Verdi's *La Traviata* on his stereo, and in the morning he sang Donizetti's *Lucia di Lammermoor* in the shower. His voice was not unpleasant. When it bled through the thin walls, Madeline and Gustavo would wake and roll toward one another and stare at each other in silence until Clifford finished his shower.

Gustavo would say, "Cliff has no future in opera, but I do not mind his singing."

"No," Madeline would say, "I don't mind it, either."

Stirred by the dark romance of Donizetti, Gustavo would grab Madeline by the waist and draw her to him and kiss her until she moaned, until his erection was hard on her thigh, until he moaned, too, and slipped inside her to make love slowly but forcefully, the music of Donizetti echoing in his head.

Dear Gustavo...

Madeline stumbles over nothing on the cold mud of Via Veleno. She falls to her knees, catching herself with her hands. Her knees bruise, her hands sting. She weeps. She tells herself it is only the bruising and the stinging that causes her pain.

In Bagno di Tristezza the post office is just around the corner from the market and two short blocks from the cafe. These are the only places Madeline knows. She does not care to know the others – for example, what sits behind those desolate stucco and concrete façades pressed shoulder to shoulder along the highway – the highway that serves as the heart of this Florentine suburb but seems to only lead in or out, never to. Grim façades. Reeking of neglect and old delusions, lost fortunes: The industrialism of Florence could have spread east but didn't. Thus the pitiable Italian suburb, Bagno di Tristezza.

Madeline likes the name – Bath of Sorrow – but does not like the place. Each morning on her way to the post office she passes through its gloomy heart. Literally reeking of resentment. A real stench of plugged sewers and piled garbage and rotting gardens. The disillusionment and futility visible, too, in the unwatered patches of grass and chipped paint and wild skinny dogs and yellowed laundry flapping between the gray choked buildings.

In a building choked gray, Massimo stands on his balcony and unbuttons the jacket of his uniform. He sees Madeline walking below and stops breathing. He watches her pass, hears her shoes falling hard on the cold mud road, beating out the rhythm of her rage. A policeman knows many things but especially this: Rage is a fat thing and, depending upon the magnitude of the crime, the predisposition of the victim, rage can be not only fat but insatiable. It swells inside the heart, feeding on the freshest wound, then the wounds that never healed, then the nearly forgotten scars. And when rage has swallowed all of the old pains, it will spit them up and start all over again, gnawing its way to outrageous proportions until it is virtually the only tenant the heart can accommodate. And so he suspects, he knows, that for Madeline there is the cafe for espresso and the market for groceries and the post office for letters, and her fat fat rage moving her inexorably forward.

Massimo leans against the balcony railing to watch Madeline disappear around the corner. He does not ask for it but it is there: his desire, cock hard against the hard metal, pressing harder as he closes his eyes and imagines Madeline naked beneath him, needing. Imagines fucking her so perfectly he drowns, dissolves in her saltwater. Imagines so acutely that his knees weaken and he grabs hold of the railing and its hard chill awakens him to the gray sky and the clean, sharp-edged cuffs of his jacket: Nothing, he thinks, he knows, should be so tidy.

He looks at his watch. Knows where Madeline will be in fifteen minutes, an hour, three hours...

– five –

The post office is a dim musty room with an ancient beaten oak counter and two female clerks who are taciturn and cold, who move as if they alone have discovered the abstractness of time and thus believe their own time is infinite and to hell with non-believers. The waiting lines are tediously long: Italian businessmen with big important letters, girls with scented envelopes of pink or blue or lavender, housewives with parcels and simple white notes, and the occasional tourist (passing through or lost, never here by choice; in Bagno di Tristezza, what is there to tour?) with stacks of postcards depicting the great art of Italy.

Madeline waits. Waiting is an art she has mastered.

When her turn arrives she hands the clerk two letters and one postcard and watches the young woman shuffle through them, tally the postage, then somberly state the price in Italian: *Something-something-something-something lire.*

Madeline's left eye twitches in irritation. Nevertheless, she smiles brightly and digs into the pocket of her coat and pulls out a worn slip of paper and hands it to the clerk.

Io sono sorda. Per favore, me lo scriva.

The clerk reads the note, looks up and simultaneously gives Madeline an expression of recognition and apology. She carefully writes the sum on a notepad and slides it toward Madeline who nods once, then places the lire, bill by bill, coin by coin, on the counter. When Madeline reaches the total, the clerk raises her hand, slides the money into the cash drawer and pastes stamps on each letter. Madeline smiles brightly and nods. The clerk smiles too, though with pity, and hands the note to Madeline who carefully tucks it into her pocket and walks away.

Io sono sorda. Per favore, me lo scriva.

I am deaf. Please, write it down for me.

Madeline is not deaf. But she knows that what little Italian she has picked up since her arrival is useless against the impatience of this suburb's proletariat. They will take their own sweet time, but they will not let their time be taken by anyone else – particularly an American who is young enough and, they assume, rich enough, to have crossed an ocean in which they have only stood.

Bagno di Tristezza, Italy
December 3

Dear Krissy:

I'm enclosing a postcard of Michelangelo's *The Creation of Adam* from the Sistine Chapel. That's Adam on the left, complete except for a soul. Look at the way he reaches toward God. He doesn't seem to be trying too hard, does he? No. God is trying hard. God is reaching beyond Himself, trying to put a soul into Adam. Adam will take the soul, of course, but it's obvious he wouldn't be too upset if God changed His mind at the last minute. He wouldn't weep. He'd shrug his massive shoulders and say, "Oh, well. At least I still have my looks."

Now see the woman huddled beneath God's left arm. She's beautiful, isn't she? Some say she's Mary, some say she's Eve. I say she's both. She's the Virgin, she's the Mother, she's the Whore. Soon after God shoves a soul into Adam, He will hand Eve over to Adam. She knows this. See how she clutches the arm of God? See how she looks at Adam? Her eyes are full of fear. Or is she merely startled, rendered speechless, musicless, by Adam's beauty, afraid she'll vanish altogether beside his unforgiveable radiance? Why the hell would Eve want to leave the comfort of Heaven to live with a man who doesn't give a damn whether he receives a soul or not? That's the question I ask. Now I ask that question every day. I look at Eve and try and try and try to understand.

Your loving sister,
Maddi

Bagno di Tristezza, Italy
December 3

Dear Ms. Thomas:

I am fully aware that my exhibition of recent drawings was to begin today. But as you can see by the postmark I am in Italy, which is nowhere near Chicago unless one considers distance relative to the entire cosmos, which I do often consider now, having so much time to stand and gaze at the sky and dream about such things. But never mind that. The point is, I am in Italy and you are in Chicago wondering what the hell you are going to do with your bare gallery walls now that I've defaulted on my contract with Chance Gallery. Sorry about that. These things happen. Surely you must have known this when you accepted your job as gallery director. Still, I do apologize. I'm certain all this has caused you some senseless grief. But grief, too, is relative. Einstein never discussed the relatively of grief, but it exists. You grieve simply because an artist you met only once reneged on a contract. To you that contract was insurance, correct? You believed that because I signed it you would most certainly have my drawings on your walls for the month of December. Your walls are bare. You grieve. I grieve because my husband also defaulted on a contract. To me that contract was insurance that he would most certainly love me for the rest of my life (or his, whichever came last). I am alone now. I grieve. I grieve but I am already taking measures to alleviate my grief. My grief is enormous. My grief is so great it now goes by another name: Fury. Fury is a good word. I am furious in Italy. You are grieving in Chicago. Life is that way.

Sincerely,
Madeline Rivera

Bagno di Tristezza, Italy
December 3

Dear Cliff:

I searched all over this damned place for a postcard of Michelangelo's *The Creation of Eve* but to no avail. Who wants to look at Eve pleading with a belligerent God to make her as beautiful as Adam who, even while sleeping, outshines her with a beauty that transcends God?

So here is *The Last Judgment* instead, ubiquitous in this hellish Florence suburb where everyone, it seems, loves revenge.

Patiently waiting,
Madeline

Massimo watches Madeline exit the post office. Feels the familiar quickening of his heart, heat pumping to the face and cock. He checks his watch, enters the time in a small leather notebook. Closes his eyes. Quietly hums Donizetti's *Una Furtiva Lagrima*.

– six –

The tower is cold today.

Stefano says it's only the beginning. "One week, Signora, two week more, and the cold come *here,*" he says, pointing to his narrow chest.

Madeline shrugs her shoulders and starts to walk away. Stefano grabs her arm and spins her around.

"Okay for you!" he shouts fiercely. He is drunk again, his breath betraying his rotting stomach. "Okay for you! But I am old, signorina. My wife, old. My dog, old. And now is the *l'invierno...l'invierno...l'invierno!*"

He looks for Madeline to translate.

She stares at him dumbly.

He slaps a hand to his weathered forehead and gives her a slight shake. *"L'INVIERNO!"* he screams, jabbing a thumb toward the sky and pretending to shiver.

"Winter?" Madeline asks.

"Sí, winter!" Stefano mumbles something damning under his breath. "So, now the winter, *sí?"*

"Yes."

"Yes! And the winter kill all that is old. This is true. This is life. And I am old. My Angelina, old. My Topi, old. So the winter kill us and we die."

Madeline pulls her arm free from Stefano's knotty hand. His withered body sways back and forth on spindly legs. She says, "We are all dying, Stefano. Winter is as good a reason as any," and walks away.

"Non capisco! Non capisco!" Stefano calls with the desperation of a man who believes he has just been given an indecipherable clue to his own mortality. "Please, Signorina Rivera! I do not understand!"

Madeline tosses her head over her shoulder. *"Non importa,* Stefano.*"*

She passes through the gate and into the garden.

Behind her, Stefano curses in Italian.

To reach the tower Madeline must enter through the south door of the villa that opens into Stefano's kitchen. She must turn right and climb the fourteen stone steps to the second floor. She must turn left and open a door to one of the enormous rooms and walk through the maze of hat and shoe boxes and dress racks and cedar chests and armoires to get to the thirty wooden steps that lead to the tower door. In the tower the centuries are acute.

Four hundred years it has stood on this hill like a sentinel staring out over an immutable valley, expecting thieves. There is nothing to steal but the silence. Even the seasons do not really alter the landscape – a subtle shifting from green to brown in winter, a falling of leaves, yet nothing the spring will not rectify.

Dear Gustavo: Listen. It is quiet here. Deathly quiet in this tower. So quiet I can hear the blood pulsing through my veins, hear it in my left ear, then my right – when I choose to listen. I do not choose to listen often; I am afraid the blood will stop. And I can hear myself sigh. So startling to hear a sigh in this cold quiet tower that I think it must be someone else I hear, some foolish ghost sighing for you. Certainly not me. I do not sigh for you. I hate you.

Four hundred years.

This is what Stefano tells Madeline again and again like an insidious warning, as if he believes her presence could somehow bring the stones down. But Madeline does not doubt the tower's age. There are the walls: three feet thick, a weary beige – the color of Missouri sand – and each and every sharp edge caused by the stonecutter's haste gone now, erased by the swelling years of soft rains and wind. The stones have settled against one another so perfectly that the new grout seems an unnecessary precaution, a cosmetic treatment to appease those who fear this ancient citadel will crumble tomorrow if left to its own devices.

It is a square tower, not round as Madeline imagined before she found her way to the villa over the cold mud roads, inevitably found her way to Stefano standing already drunk at the wooden gate, his blind wife's hair loose and blowing wild that chilly gray autumn afternoon.

Late autumn. The second year after Gustavo and Madeline were married. Trees had already emptied their branches onto the lawns, and the air was cold and had no scent, and the sun seemed to shine from a farther distance than before. Mornings usually began gray and then turned blue in the afternoon. But sometimes Madeline would wake in the yellow bedroom drenched in a shifting pool of light and look out to see a cerulean sky, purer and more brilliant than any color she could buy in a tube or mix on a palette. Beautiful late autumn mornings. And on one of them she kissed Gustavo awake and said, "Let's go for a walk."

"It's cold, Maddi."

"No, it's beautiful. Look!" She opened the window and the cool scentless air pushed its way into the room that was too hot and smelled of the night's wine and cigarettes and sex. "It's been so long since we went for a walk together."

Gustavo turned on his side, away from her, and pulled the blankets over his head.

Madeline nudged him with her foot. "Please, Gustavo. Go for a walk with me."

"No. I want to sleep. I played until one o'clock last night."

"I know. I was there. You were beautiful."

"I am tired, Maddi."

Madeline sighed and looked out beyond the barren trees, at the sky humming with color: a great blue symphony of light made visible, almost audible. She wanted to be under that sky. She wanted to be under its immense weightlessness, the open notes rising to a crescendo that too soon would descend as the gray oppressiveness of winter took hold. She wanted to be under that sky with Gustavo. She wanted Gustavo to want to be under it with her.

Madeline stared down at the motionless lump of Gustavo on the bed and reached out and yanked the blankets off his naked body and threw them onto the floor.

Gustavo screamed.

Madeline grinned.

Gustavo shook his fist and said, "I'll kill you," but his black eyes were laughing.

"You could never kill me, Gustavo."

Gustavo arched his eyebrows and folded his hands behind his head with comic nonchalance. "Sure I could."

Madeline shook her head. "No, Gustavo. Murder isn't in your nature. There are killers and there are victims. You are a victim."

"Wrong," Gustavo said flatly, loudly. Then he growled, baring his teeth like a rabid dog, and threw Madeline a ridiculous childish glower. She stifled a laugh. For a full minute they faced one another, lips pursed, quivering with amusement. Suddenly Gustavo leaped toward Madeline and grabbed her wrists and pulled her down onto the bed, and she did not fight him but went tumbling over the cold sheets and warm skin, screaming and laughing, each scream trailing into laughter.

Gustavo pressed his body over Madeline's and pinned her to the bed and snarled, "I am a killer, I am a killer." His accent – *I am a keeler* – only made the words more absurd, and Madeline laughed harder, wriggling beneath him like captured prey, glad to be captured, to feel his skin over hers – skin still brown from summer and smooth over the hard muscles and smelling sweet and acrid all at once.

"I am a killer," Gustavo said again, then curled his wide hands around Madeline's neck. She felt them grow tighter but kept laughing, knowing Gustavo would not make them tighten more.

Gustavo grinned. "See? See?"

"Oh, yes, I see," laughed Madeline. "I see that I was right. You're no killer."

Gustavo took his hands from Madeline's neck and laid them on her shoulders and kissed her quickly on the forehead and cheek and mouth and chin. "Okay," he said, "I am not a killer. But what are you?"

"Not a victim."

"Then you are a killer."

"Yes."

"Could you kill me?"

"Yes."

"I don't believe you."

"Believe me."

Gustavo cocked his head to one side and smiled. "But you love me. How could you kill me?"

"I don't know how, but I could."

"For what reason?"

"Betrayal," Madeline said, surprised by her answer, surprised that it came so quickly and simply, without thought or rumination.

Gustavo sneered.

Madeline nodded. "It's true." She reached up and tried wrapping her hands around Gustavo's neck, but it was a thick brown neck and Madeline's hands were pale and small against it. So she placed her thumbs over his jugular vein and said, "If you ever betray me, if you leave me for another woman, I'll kill you."

Gustavo smiled. "You won't kill me. You love me."

Madeline pressed her thumbs into Gustavo's flesh. "I'll kill you."

Gustavo smiled. "You won't."

"I will," said Madeline, and pressed harder.

Gustavo's face began to redden. His smile flickered. "But, Maddi, you love me."

Madeline pressed harder.

Gustavo's eyes watered. His voice broke as he screamed. "MADELINE!" and tore her hands away and shoved them hard against her breasts. He hovered over her, his face close, his breath coming quick and heavy and feverish from his flared nostrils, his black eyes dry and red and full of fear. Madeline had never seen Gustavo's fear, and when she recognized it, saw it in his eyes – that were black, which were beautiful, which she loved – she began to cry.

Gustavo did not cry. His body grew still and rigid as a corpse, and just as heavy: not a muscle twitching, not even a shifting of his eyes – that were black, that were beautiful, that she loved – that were full now of a fear she'd never seen before and so were foreign, those eyes, black stones made impenetrable and strange because of the fear they now possessed.

"Gustavo Rivera," Madeline cried, "never, never, never betray me."

Gustavo searched Madeline's face with his black eyes, then turned his head away and laid it on her shoulder. She waited for him to speak. Her hands moved along his back – over the stiff muscles, the soft skin cold now and damp – her blind hands groping the stiffness and coldness and dampness, searching for absolution.

Finally Gustavo said quietly, calmly, with certitude: "I will never betray you, Madeline Rivera."

And Madeline Rivera believed him. Then.

The tower is thirty feet wide by thirty feet long, with a high ceiling. The ceiling is so high and so dark Madeline notices it only when she wakes in the morning and finds it above her: blood-red tiles and timbers blackened with age. At night the tower is dark and the ceiling is dark. If Madeline wakes in the night she does not see the blood-red tiles or blackened timbers, only the pervasive darkness as if it were the sky above her head: starless and infinite and godless. And when Madeline looks down – in the long afternoons when she looks down and watches her feet measure off the distance between walls – she sees the same blood-red tiles darkened and pocked and polished by a hundred heels which have paced this tower four hundred years. Paced it back and forth, back and forth, as if the tower's width corresponded precisely to the length of each person's waiting.

Dear Gustavo: Without music there is blood in the veins and breath like a sigh and heels pounding against the blood-red tiles day after day after day after day.

There is one square window each in the north, south and west walls of the tower. In the east wall there is one door by which to enter the tower. The windows are high up in the high walls, so high that Madeline must crane her neck in order to look out. And when she does she can see only the sky – not even the red tile roofs of the other villas in the valley, not even the blood spilling over the horizon before dusk, not even the tops of trees. Only the sky, a white-gray square of light in the day and indigo at night with a ghost of a moon through the clouds, when there is a moon.

Madeline can go for days without wanting more, days with only the square of light or square of dark and a roomful of silence. So many days when that's enough. But when that is not enough, when her loneliness gathers into one square then another, pushing against the suffocating boundaries of stone, pushing hard, it screams:

Dear Gustavo!

Just below the south window, cut into the thick stone, is a small window seat cushioned with a faded blue pillow. The seat is also high, so high that Madeline would not have known it was for sitting were it not for the round deep imprints of someone's ass on the faded blue pillow. It is not comfortable sitting so high on a seat so small, but it is a good place to write letters.

From here Madeline can see the valley filled with mist in the morning, see the distant villas, the cold mud roads winding through the brown hills, the neat olive groves, and far away the steeple of the small church which peals its melancholy notes each morning and noon and evening to tell Madeline and everyone else in the valley that time is passing.

Bagno di Tristezza, Italy
December 4

Dear Cliff:

Time is passing. It's the 4th of December. I am waiting and waiting and waiting. It's winter and cold and I'm alone in the tower. Sometimes when the rain comes and there is nowhere else for me to go but from one cold wall to another, I feel as if the world has vanished while I wasn't looking, and it's just me. Me and Gustavo. I know he's alive because I can still smell him. I wake from a dream that's more like a memory and that's all I smell: Gustavo's skin, like leaves, like early autumn when the leaves have just fallen, before they begin to rot. A smell not at all like death, but like the heavy accumulation of life, rich and erotic. I used to love the smell of autumn, but now it only signals the end of things: the end of summer, the end of warmth, the end of another year. I don't miss Gustavo, it's just that I dream about him sometimes when the rain comes and I'm tired of pacing the tower and my bed is the warmest place to be, and so I lay in bed all day sleeping and dreaming and waking to the smell of leaves like Gustavo's skin. Find him.

Madeline

Madeline sits in the high window seat. There is a notebook on her lap. Staring up at her is a perfectly white, perfectly blank page. White as the silence in the tower; blank as the winter sky beyond the window. Below her the mud roads are dark and shining from the rain that falls from the blank winter sky. Rain invisible until it reaches the brown landscape of the valley and drapes it in a thin watery veil, obscuring only the lines between one thing and the next. Thus the world seems simultaneously near and distant.

Across the valley, on a road alongside an olive grove silent now except for the moaning of wind through gnarled branches, Massimo removes his police cap and sets it beside him on the car seat and rolls down the window. He raises his binoculars and looks out across the valley at the tower of a villa, at its window glowing warmly in the descending dusk, at the woman sitting there inside, peering back at him, it seems – her gray eyes emptied by indefinable sadness – though he knows it is not him she sees. The moment he realizes this, he feels something tear in his breast. The first rent. And he sighs, "Ah, *sí, sí, sí!*"

On the driveway outside the front gate, Topi limps forward into the rain. Her head droops and her tail droops and her sad legs step slowly, slowly onto the cold

39

shining mud. A few yards later she stops, not suddenly but imperceptibly, as if her single purpose for moving forward was lost earlier and only now is she aware of its absence. She stands at the end of the driveway, moving neither forward nor backward, moving not at all for a long time. Her balding coat gathers moisture. She does not even bother to shiver. Suddenly her head swings over her shoulder and she quickly turns and just as quickly cowers. And there is Stefano staggering toward her.

Madeline cannot hear Stefano from her high perch inside the tower, but she can see his violent gesturing, his head rolling around on his neck like a gyroscope. He swiftly steps toward Topi and aims a boot at her rib cage. Topi dodges by collapsing her legs and dropping hard onto the mud beneath her. Stefano's boot swings out and upward, so full of the momentum of his anger that the whole of his body is lifted off the ground and dropped onto the mud. Topi takes advantage of Stefano's supine position and hobbles out of view, tail tucked between her legs. Stefano climbs to his feet. He turns to look after Topi, then buries his head in his hands.

Madeline looks down at the white blank page.

Bagno di Tristezza
December 5

Dear Dr. Frederick:
You said, "Some days are better than others." How long was I in therapy? A month and a half? I'm sure it was a month and a half. 2 sessions per week for 6 weeks. $85 per session. That's $1020, right? Sure I'm right. Contrary to life, math is an

absolute science. Six weeks, $1020, and the only thing you told me that made sense was, "Some days are better than others." Yet on this particular day as I stood in line the post office pretending to be deaf, it suddenly occurred to me that we, you and I, approach life from very different angles. We do not see eye to eye, Dr. Frederick. There you are, looking at the glass, smiling, stroking your stereotypical goatee and telling anyone who's willing to pay to hear, "*Voilà!* The glass is half full." And here I am, chin in hand, sighing, looking at the glass and flicking a cold finger against it to hear what it has to say, and it says, *gratis,* "I am half empty." Now, who's to say who is right and who is wrong? You have your reality; I have mine. So I tell you now: Some days are *not* better than others. (Were they ever? Doesn't one great lie discount all conclusions?) I am living day to day as you suggested but not *because* you suggested. I am living day to day because I must. Therefore. Therefore now: Some days are worse than others, and they are all bad.

Madeline Rivera

— seven —

The sixth of December.

The rain falls.

Madeline lights a cigarette and stares off at the northern hills where smoke rises inscrutable as the past. Rises like rage, fat with a life of its own.

"Evil all here and there."

Madeline turns. "What?"

"You feel?" Angelina asks. "The air smell with evil."

Angelina plants a wooden pieta in the patch of weeds behind the villa, spade digging violently into the half-frozen earth. Her wet hair is plastered against her forehead and cheeks, and her thin white nightgown becomes transparent, exposing her pubic hair and bulging stomach and large sagging breasts. Each time her spade digs into the black soil, she lets loose a grunt and mumbles, *"Requiescat in pace."*

The pieta rests on its side. Jesus, dead in Mary's arms, gathers rain in the hollow of his wooden loincloth.

And here comes Stefano, lurching out of his flat, holding a bottle of Chianti in one hand, waving his arms and slurring his wearisome curses at Angelina. The wine spills over his undershirt and trousers. He is oblivious to the rain, unlike Madeline who shivers against the stone wall of the villa, teeth chattering. She pulls her scarf from her head and tilts her head back and opens her mouth and inhales the cold rain until she chokes on it.

Stefano stops short of the spade's downward sweep and wails to the heavens, *"Mio giardino! Il mio bello giardino!"*

Angelina tosses a spadeful of wet soil onto his feet.

Stefano stares down at the hole, which is now a foot deep, and sticks out his lower lip in a quivering pout. *"Pomodori,"* he sighs, *"zucchini..."*

"No," says Angelina, digging harder, grunting louder. "No *Pomodori*, no *zucchini*. Evil! *Capisce?"*

Stefano, pained and confused, narrows his eyes at her. "Evil?"

"Evil, evil, evil," hisses Angelina.

"Eh?"

"Cattivo, Stefano! *Come tu!"*

"Ah," Stefano says, nodding, and takes another swig of Chianti.

Angelina blindly indicates the old man with a jerk of her head. "Rotting pocket of evil." She lays down her spade and searches for the pieta. She kisses it once and props it up in the hole and packs the dirt that has turned to mud around its base to hold wooden Mary and dead Jesus upright. *"Requiescat in pace, requiescat in pace, requiescat in pace..."*

At the old musician's funeral, Madeline put her lips to Gustavo's ear and whispered: "What do you love most in the world?"

Without taking his eyes from the corpse, Gustavo whispered back, "Music."

The priest sang: *"Dignare, Domine, die isto, sine peccato nos custodire..."*

"Why?" asked Madeline.

"It is necessity," replied Gustavo.

"Necessity for what?"

"For life."

"...miserere nostri! miserere nostri!..."

"That's ridiculous."

"No, it is not ridiculous. *¿Que es una vida sin musica? Nada. Nada!* Every day I play my violin. Every night I dream of notes on a staff. In my head I hear the music always. Music is what I make the most best." He nodded at the choir. "And when I am not making music, I listen to others make and sing. You know this is true."

"Yes, I know it," Madeline whispered sadly.

"So you see," Gustavo insisted, "music is my definition. Maybe only a part of my definition, but I cannot remember my life without it. And so without it I would not be who I am, correct? For example, who would you be without your painting?"

"I don't know. It seems I've always painted."

"Yes!"

The priest sang: *"Judex crederis esse venturus..."* Beautiful.

Madeline said, "Gustavo, who would you be without me?"

"I would be the person I was before I met you."

"That's an evil thing to say."

"I do not believe in evil."

"Then what do you believe in?"

"Music."

"Nothing else?"

"There is nothing else."

Madeline slipped a hand between Gustavo's thighs and slid it along the soft gabardine up to his cock, and pressed gently, rhythmically, then rubbed until the gabardine swelled to an unripe pear. Gustavo moaned.

Madeline grinned: "That's what I believe in."

In the square tower Madeline turns around the painting. Stands back to look at it. Gustavo's face stares back at her, somber and intense and beautiful.

She walks to the armoire and opens it up and removes the drawings and paintings inside. She props them against the walls. There are thirty, forty, fifty in various sizes and media. All rendered meticulously. Each and every detail captured on the paper or canvas. When the armoire is empty Madeline stands in the middle of the room. She revolves slowly in place. Everywhere she looks Gustavo's image looks back at her: his face smiling or serious, his body naked or clothed, his hands open or fisted, his cock soft or erect.

Dear Gustavo: You are beautiful. Because I know this, you should belong to me.

Madeline revolves: a moon centered in its own universe, trapped by a savage momentum. Her eyes glance from one wall to the next: Gustavo's faces bleed into each another, his bodies dance and stand still and dress and undress and become aroused and disinterested. He is black and white, he is color. He is watching Madeline admire his beauty, and Madeline can sense him laughing at her. His black eyes shine with laughter. She begins to sweat. Nausea rises from her navel to her throat. It is suddenly difficult to breathe.

Then she remembers the nightmare:

She is standing at the edge of a frozen river. It is a white river. The sky is white. The hills on the opposite bank are white. Everything is white and frozen and bitterly cold. But she does not mind the cold: Gustavo is standing beside her. He wears a red down jacket, the one she gave him for his birthday just after they were married. The red jacket is brilliant against the frozen white landscape. Above it, Gustavo's face is brown and beautiful and smiling at her. She recognizes the smile. It is the one he wore when they met and continued to wear until they were married and wore a few months after their marriage, and then longer still but not as often. It is the smile she loved because it said he loved her. It is the smile that made her feel happy and warm and safe. And because she sees it now she smiles, too, and does not mind the cold. And because she sees it now she does not hesitate when Gustavo tells her, "Walk to the middle of the river and wait for me." The river is frozen and white and stretches for miles to the white hills on the opposite shore. She walks. With each step she takes she can feel Gustavo's smile receding behind her. With each step she takes the cold reaches deeper into her bones, and she grows less certain of her footsteps: The frozen river seems to be shifting beneath her, a vertiginous nauseating sensation. She looks down and sees cracks in the ice, hears them splintering in the cold silent white air. The cracks are multiplying. The river is breaking into hundreds of teetering ice floes, and she can feel the distance between Gustavo's smile and her own, feel the distance as if it had weight, a heavy cold distance between Gustavo's smile and her own. Thus she is cold now and afraid and cannot go further. She calls out to Gustavo, begging him to come and rescue her. But he doesn't answer. She turns her head and sees Gustavo's red jacket, bright against the white landscape, his brown face smiling a strange smile that does not warm her and does not pacify her and does not make her happy. Instead it intensifies her cold and terror. She shouts, "Gustavo, help me!" Gustavo smiles, and his smile is hideous: demonic, evil, alien —

incongruous with the beautiful black eyes and beautiful bones and beautiful brown skin. Panicking, she tells herself: *If I can make my way back to the river bank, if I can just get back to Gustavo, everything will be all right, everything will be like it was before.* But the floes have become incredibly small, the size of quarters, and she cannot get back. Everywhere she looks, the ice is breaking up. And now she can see the raging river beneath it, the river surrounding her: miles of angry black water sweeping over and around the single floe upon which she stands. And it, too, shrinks beneath her boots – her heavy boots that are useless against the cold, leaden on the thin vanishing ice. The river rages and she is sinking into its freezing waters. And then she understands: *I am drowning.* Before her head disappears beneath the black water, she sees Gustavo on the distant bank, waving at her, smiling his hideous smile, slowly opening his red jacket to reveal the many faceless women inside.

– eight –

No radio, no stereo, no television, no doorbell, no whistling teapot, no clock tick, no wind chimes, no crystal prisms, no metronome, no violin, no singing voice, no caged birds, no gurgling water, no snapping fire, no humming air.

No music.

December 7.

Blood through the veins.

And silence.

The road rises, brown and frozen and smooth except for the occasional pebble that juts sharply through mud, stabbing the thin soles of Madeline's shoes. Her only shoes. After 28 days and 84 kilometers, the black patent leather is scuffed and dull. The brass buckles do not shine. The low square heels are worn to thin wedges. Cold seeps in, but the seams are intact: The shoes are tight on Madeline's feet that carry her up the slope of the cold mud road with the steady persistent efficacy of a machine. Madeline watches her shoes moving forward. She does not have to think, *Move forward,* yet they move. Black patent shoes moving on the cold mud road. Her only shoes. A gift from Gustavo.

Madeline opened the box and saw the shoes and clapped her hands together. "They're beautiful!"

Gustavo nodded. "The woman at the shop said to me they are imported from Italy. She said they are made by hand. She said they are the best leather, the finest... *Mira!* The buckles are solid brass!"

"They must have been terribly expensive."

"The woman at the shop gave me a special price."

"Why?"

Gustavo shrugged, shifted his eyes, said, "Put them on."

Madeline put them on. She stood up and stared down at the shoes. The black patent shined. The brass buckles shined. Beautiful shoes.

Gustavo said, "Now, walk."

Madeline walked across the wooden floor of the apartment. The flat perfect heels and slick leather soles tapped upon the wood: heel-toe, heel-toe, heel-toe... Madeline spun around and walked from one end of the apartment to the other, then again, listening to the rhythm of the shoes upon the wooden floor: heel-toe, heel-toe, heel-toe... She stopped in front of Gustavo and smiled, "I could walk for miles in these shoes."

Gustavo nodded. "The woman at the shop said they would last forever."

Madeline bent down and kissed him. "Thank you."

Gustavo looked up at her thoughtfully. After a pause he said, *"De nada."*

At the top of the slope, immediately to the right, a long tall patch of reeds: leaves pale yellow and dry, stems bending in the perpetual wind and shuddering, whispering a disapproving commentary, uninformed accusations, hostile judgments. As if Madeline's thoughts were audible. They are not audible. Her lips do not move, her tongue does not curl, her vocal chords do not vibrate when she thinks, *Dear Gustavo...* And what do reeds know about pain, anyway? They sway in the wind and eat from the soil and drink from the rain and florish beneath the sun and are never

49

disappointed. The wind and the soil and the rain and the sun are constant. They will be here until the world ends. It is not the end of the world, is it?

No. Not yet.

Massimo checks his watch, starts the police car, slowly turns onto the highway that passes through Bagno di Tristezza. By now he knows the schedules of everyone in Villa Ferramo: Stefano sleeps off a hangover while Angelina waits for death by the morning fire. Topi curled in the tall dry grass along the road waits for Madeline's return. And Madeline: halfway to the post office by now, feet pounding the depth of her rage on the hard mud road, colder each day as the world descends into winter.

The police car circles the suburb, arrives at the backside of Villa Ferramo. Massimo steps out, walks by the rear flat and glances through a dusty window at Angelina sitting near the fireplace, nodding to the rattle of Stefano's snores as if in polite conversation.

He slips through the heavy wooden gate. The door lock is easily picked, and he shakes his head in reproach. He is, after all a policeman, concerned about the safety of all.

Inside the villa he climbs the fourteen stone steps to the second floor, makes his way to the tower stairs. He puts one foot on the first step. Hesitates. Something flutters inside his chest, something light and warm. Promising. Spring, he thinks. The perpetual spring of love for a woman who loves without limit, without regret. He sighs – a whisper: "Ah, *sí.*" And ascends.

The tower is cold but he does not notice, for the air is thick with Madeline's scent – hair and mouth, breasts and belly, thighs…moisture that draws him forward into the room where he stands, there, in the center of her life. He paces, back and forth back and forth on the blood-red tiles, eyes closed, inhaling whatever the room gives up of her. He stops. Gazes at the bed where she sleeps and dreams, dreams as he dreams, for he is certain now he knows her, by her scent, by her absence that swells in him a pleasant sadness.

Not the end of the world. No. Not yet.

Beyond the smug reeds, a meadow slopes downward to the lowest part of the valley where a small house sits among the oaks and pines, smoke curling from its chimney. There is no music in smoke. Only silence. And in the silence that rises and curls and dissipates in the wind: the suggestion of contentment.

Madeline pauses here on the cold mud road to gaze down at the house and the curling smoke. Waiting for someone, anyone, to exit the small house. Waiting to see the distant face of a stranger content within the silence of smoke. Madeline can smell the silence, the smoke. The valley is filled with its scent.

It is winter now, and cold. Fires burn. The valley resigns itself to the silence of smoke, and everyone is waiting.

Bagno di Tristezza, Italy
December 8

Dear Cliff:
Stefano says that when spring comes he will be happy. He will not trip his blind wife or kick his sick dog because it will be warm and he will no longer need his Chianti to numb

himself to winter, so he will be sober and happy.

Stefano lives for the coming of spring.

Why do I live? Not for spring. I cannot imagine it coming. Spring's just a word, abstract, a distant foreign place and time in which I cannot imagine myself. When Gustavo left he took with him my future: every spring, summer, autumn, winter yet to come. I have today. And tomorrow I will have today. And the day after that I will have today.

Why do I live? I live for the unknowable today when you find Gustavo and I take back my future. And because nothing is free, not even a future, here's another $500 for expenses.

Madeline

A lifetime ago, in another country, there were rules and the rules were clear:

Do not talk with your mouth full, do not talk during movies, do not talk during sermons, do not exceed the speed limit, do not run red lights, do not park in loading zones, do not drink and drive, do not serve red wine with chicken, do not arrive early to a party, do not arrive late to a symphony, do not cut in line, do not litter, do not spit on sidewalks, do not flush tampons down toilets, do not urinate in public, do not fornicate in public, do not swim immediately after eating, do not dive into shallow waters, do not stare at the sun, do not walk under ladders, do not laugh when a hearse goes by, do not wear red to a funeral, do not lie, do not steal, do not commit adultery…

Do not kill.

Clifford Beale said, "Talk to me, Madeline. Tell me what it feels like to have Gustavo gone.

Madeline lay in the yellow bedroom, naked beneath the sheets, silent.

"You need to talk about it," said Clifford Beale. "If you don't, it'll build up and explode."

Madeline's eyes were red and swollen, her lips bleeding from the gnashing of her own teeth, her face turned toward the yellow wall. By now she knew every imperfection in the plaster, the smallest lump and scratch more familiar than the back of her own hand. A single bristle left by the painter's brush said it all: the horror of the immobility of the loneliness of being left behind.

Clifford looked at the untouched tray of food and water on the nightstand. He sighed, stroked Madeline's shoulder that was cold and damp. He whispered, "Tell me, Madeline. What's it like with him gone?"

Madeline opened her mouth. Her throat was so dry, swollen, parched, that her voice had to fight its way past her tongue: "Like death."

Clifford smiled and nodded. "And what will you do now, Madeline? What will you do to get your life back?"

Madeline rolled over and stared up at Clifford who stared down at her with a desperate tenderness. She opened her mouth to speak, but no words came out.

Clifford held a glass of water to Madeline's lips, and Madeline drank from it while he brushed his fingers through her oily hair.

In another country – a lifetime ago – there were rules and the rules were clear: Do not kill. When Madeline left that other country, she left behind its rules.

Here the road is straight and flat. It passes between two small villas – one old, one new. The villas are connected by a cantilevered passageway that arches over the cold mud of Via Veleno. Tall windows are set into the north and south sides of this passageway so that the sky is visible through it, coming or going. Sometimes people walk through the passageway from the old villa to the new, from the new to the old. Sometimes these people pause at the tall windows to look down at Madeline passing beneath them on the cold mud road.

Below the red tile roof, the passageway eaves are crowded with roosting pigeons. Their white and gray excrement falls and spatters on the brown mud road. Occasionally a feather drifts down. Pigeons gaze out of red-rimmed eyes at Madeline who passes beneath them, gazing back, listening to their placid cooing. They are not songbirds, but they have their song, they have their music. Melancholy and euphonious as cellos.

Cellos... cellos... cellos...

Dvorak: *Rondo for Cello and Orchestra, Opus 94.*

Backstage at the symphony, in another country, another life:

Gustavo took Madeline by the arm and led her through a crowd of musicians preparing to go on stage. It was spring. Madeline wore yellow. Bright yellow. The color of daffodils. The musicians wore black. Funereal but elegant: men in black tuxedos and stiff white shirts, women in black gowns. Musicians quietly chatting, instruments in hand. Some silently fingering notes, eyes half closed. All of them handsome and lovely in black, but no one beautiful except Gustavo who kissed Madeline on the cheek and led her through the crowd of musicians to a middle-aged man with blond hair and green eyes and a straight thin nose which he looked down when he spoke to the musicians who surrounded him. As Gustavo drew near, the musicians parted. The blond man gazed at Gustavo, then at Madeline. He almost smiled.

"Bernard Allande," said Gustavo, bowing his head with enough precision to convey deference but not obsequiousness. "I would like to introduce to you my wife, Madeline Rivera."

"Then do it!" snapped Bernard Allande, then smiled suddenly and took Madeline's hand in his and kissed the tip of her middle knuckle. "Such a pleasure to make your acquaintance," he whispered, his French accent bastardized from traveling too long in too many foreign countries.

Madeline politely retrieved her hand. "The pleasure is mine."

"Bernard is our resident artist from Paris," said Gustavo. "He will play with the symphony for six months, and tonight he is the featured cellist."

"Ah," said Madeline.

"Do you love the cello?" asked Bernard Allande.

"Yes," said Madeline, "very much."

"More than the violin?"

Madeline paused: a mistake: Gustavo's black eyes narrowed. She could not take back the pause, though she tried. "No, not more really, not..."

"Madeline is a painter," Gustavo said coolly. "She does not know music."

"I know what I like," said Madeline, "and what I don't like."

Bernard Allande's green eyes danced. "Then do you like Dvorak?"

"I love Dvorak."

"That's good," said Bernard. "Tonight we do Dvorak. *Rondo for Cello and Orchestra.* The cello, of course, played expertly by me. You are familiar with this rondo?"

"Yes."

"And do you love it?"

"I do."

"Then I will dedicate tonight's performance to you, Madeline Rivera."

Gustavo's shoulders stiffened.

Bernard continued, "I will look into the audience and find your pleasant yellow dress and I will smile. My smile will serve as proof of my dedication. To you, Madeline Rivera."

Madeline stared at Bernard Allande. She stared at him while studying Gustavo out of the corner of her eye. Gustavo was staring at Bernard too, with a face full of darkness. Such a strange darkness in Gustavo's face. Madeline had not seen such darkness before. Not in Gustavo's face. Not in anyone's face. And because she had not seen it, she could not comprehend precisely its meaning. Unhappiness, yes, that much was certain. And yet...

Unhappiness was not precise enough. Precision was everything. Precisely...

But there was no time for precision.

"Thank you," Madeline told Bernard Allande, and smiled weakly.

Gustavo took Madeline by the arm and led her away as Bernard Allande said loudly, vaguely: "Such a pleasant yellow dress!"

And so: *Rondo for Cello and Orchestra, Opus 94.*

Madeline sat in the audience, fourth row, dead center – lovely in her pleasant yellow dress. Gustavo sat on the stage, third chair of the first violins – beautiful in his black tuxedo. Bernard Allande sat center stage, to the left of the conductor, isolated, singled out from the orchestra for his great, though waning talent – handsome but not beautiful in his black tuxedo.

And so: *Rondo for Cello and Orchestra, Opus 94.*

The conductor raised his baton.

True to his word, Bernard Allande glanced up from the cello between his knees and let his eyes roam over the audience until they landed upon Madeline in her pleasant yellow dress. He dipped his head and smiled, then his eyes closed and he was lost inside Dvorak.

Madeline returned his smile: a reflex, a mistake. Her gray eyes shifted to Gustavo whose black eyes had also found her pleasant yellow dress, then found her face, her gray eyes, and pierced them with his own.

Madeline's smile died on her lips.

After the concert Gustavo did not speak to Madeline. Did not speak to her for days.

"I did nothing," she protested. "I was polite. I simply told Bernard Allande that I love Dvorak. I told him I love Dvorak because I do. Dvorak. Not Bernard Allande. You. Not Bernard Allande. I did nothing, Gustavo. Nothing. Speak to me. Speak to me!"

When Gustavo finally spoke, his first words were, "What have you done with my blue shirt? I cannot find my blue shirt."

Past the old and new villas split apart, Via Veleno curves toward the left then rises again. It is not a steep slope but gradual. It rises, gradually, until the cold mud road becomes a cold paved road. Gray pavement that shines black in the rain.

It is raining. The pavement shines black. Madeline walks through the shallow puddles in her black patent shoes. The water seeps through the seams. Her socks are wet, her feet are wet. And cold. Her toes grow numb. She curls them as she walks, trying to force blood back into them. But the curling takes an effort, is not mechanical, and causes her pace to slow, so she stops curling her toes to maintain her mechanical pace. The rain on her face, on her long black coat, on the black woolen scarf over her head does not bother her. It is a light rain, like mist drawn by the earth from the sky. A gray sky. The color of Madeline's eyes and just as empty.

Dear Gustavo: My eyes are empty. They mirror my soul. My soul is an empty vessel. The vessel is cracked. There are pieces missing. You are those pieces.
Heel-toe, heel-toe, heel-toe...

Here is the small stone church with its single bell that peals its melancholy notes each morning and noon and evening to tell Madeline and everyone else in the valley that time is passing.

Time is passing.

December 9.

The church steeple pierces the gray empty sky, its iron cross vanished in the falling mist. An old priest with hunched shoulders and a shrunken face steps out through the heavy wooden door of the church and shuffles down the cobbled walkway. He opens the iron gate of the churchyard just as Madeline passes. Madeline nods at him. He looks into Madeline's eyes and sees they are empty. He whispers, *"La madonna nera!"* and crosses himself and wheels around and quickly shuffles back up the cobbled walkway to the heavy wooden door that he opens, then pauses to glance over his shoulder and whisper, *"La madonna della morte!"* before hurrying inside.

Stefano calls out, *"La madonna nera!"*

Madeline pauses at the garden gate.

Stefano takes a swig of Chianti and staggers forward, grinning treacherously. "Black madonna, I have no *spavento!"*

Madeline stares at him. *"Spavento?"*

"Sí, spavento...spavento..." Stefano opens his eyes wide in mock terror and raises his hands as if to deflect a blow. *"SPAVENTO!"*

"Fear?" Madeline asks.

"Sí, sí, fear. I have no fear of you."

Madeline shrugs and opens the gate.

Stefano grabs the wood with his knotty fingers and slams the gate shut. He leans toward Madeline, bloodshot eyes darting from side to side. "The people who live here along Via Veleno, they have fear of you. They see you walk every morning in your black, *andata e ritorno,* to and from, to and from," says Stefano marching in place. "The people say you carry *la morte* inside your heart. *La morte...*death. They say, *La* *madonna nera. La madonna della morte,* and they have fear. They have fear you bring death to them, to the children, to the animals, to the olive trees. But I say no, it is *l'opposto. Il contrario.* See? My Topi is still alive."

Madeline looks at Topi, who sits trembling on her haunches beneath a dead olive tree.

"The people along Via Veleno are right," says Madeline. "I do carry death in my heart. *La morte* in my heart. But not for them. No, there's no room in my heart for so many deaths. There's room for only one."

Stefano's mouth opens in surprise. A belch escapes. "My death?" he asks fearfully. *"La mia morte?"*

Madeline laughs quietly and uncurls Stefano's fingers one by one and opens the gate and passes through.

Stefano screams, "Signora Rivera! Tell me, please! This one death, it is mine?"

Madeline disappears into the villa.

Stefano cocks his head sideways and frowns at his shoes. *"La madonna nera,"* he whispers and takes a swig of Chianti and belches. *"La madonna della morte."*

Winter sinks into the valley.

Time is passing: December 10.
Beyond the church, olive trees glisten.

The woman stands on a wooden ladder, her round body heaving against her thin brown coat. The coat is old. Too short in the arms and torn at the seams, held together with safety pins. Her thick legs are covered with black stockings. The stockings are old. Here and there a white splotch of flesh shows through the coarse black weave. She wears men's shoes. They are old shoes. The leather is as thick and stiff and hard as the woman's face. The soles are cracked. When the woman walks through the grass, from one gnarled tree to the next, icy dew fills her shoes and her feet grow numb. She wears no gloves, is perhaps forty, forty-five, but her hands would tell you eighty: They are more swollen and twisted than the trees she cleans of their black fruit. There is a rag tied to her waist because her fingers bleed always, always bleed. The grove is nearly picked clean and the rag is stained by her bleeding fingers.

She tries to hum. The melody catches in her swollen throat and she coughs. She coughs and coughs. She wraps an old green scarf tighter around her neck and tries to hum. Instead she coughs. Coughs until her face is as red as her bleeding fingers. Until tears stream from her eyes and she can no longer see the black fruit on the trees. Until her legs tremble on the top rung of the ladder. Until the ladder falls.

Madeline walks by on her way the post office, her ears already tuned toward the grove, anticipating accidental music. The grove is silent.

¿Que es una vida sin musica?

Madeline pauses on the wet black pavement of Via Veleno and lights a cigarette. She squints through the smoke and looks out across this valley of crumbling villas and olive groves and cold mud roads. She listens. The silence is deafening.

What is a life without music?

She looks toward the olive grove. Flicks her cigarette into the wet grass where it hisses and dies. She climbs the iron fence surrounding the olive grove and walks between the rows of gnarled trees, the scent of ripe olives rising from the cold earth. She sees the fallen ladder, the silent lump of a woman. She rushes forward and kneels among the black olives spilled thickly upon the ground. She touches the woman's face. It's cold. Colder than the mud of Via Veleno. She loosens the thin green scarf around the woman's neck and presses two fingers against the cold neck. There is no pulse. She presses harder. There is no pulse. She withdraws her fingers and looks into the woman's eyes that are half open, staring into a distance so vast they see nothing at all. Madeline kisses the woman's eyes one by one, then removes the black woolen scarf around her own head and carefully spreads it over the woman's face. She stands.

What is a life without music?

The grove is silent.

What is a life without music?

Blood through the veins.

What is a life without music?

Madeline lifts her gray empty eyes to the gray empty sky and screams: "Gu-sta-vo!"

Her voice echoes over the valley and the cold mud roads and crumbling villas.

Birds everywhere take flight.

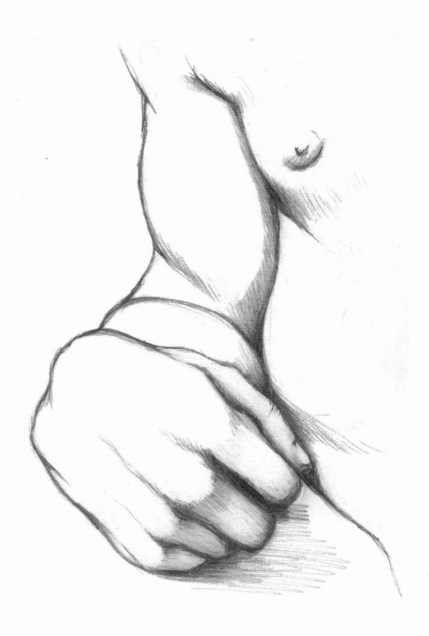

III. Intermezzo
Capriccio for solo violin

In Paris it rains. The sky is low. So low that all buildings are reduced to a single height: the level at which they meet the descending sky. The monuments and towers appear incomplete, the interrupted dreams of architects – spires and crowns and arches dissolved in the wet gray sky. All of Paris is wet and gray. A pale wash of thinned ink. Sky, buildings, pavement...all gray and bleeding together like ink spilled on a wet page. But it is just the phenomenon of rain.

Gustavo likes the rain. It flushes the streets empty and silent. In silence he can hear the music inside his head without distraction.

What is this music?

Capriccio for solo violin.

It does not exist except inside his head. He walks in the rain, along empty silent streets, and hears the caprice. The fingers of his left hand twitch unconsciously, imagining themselves dancing upon the taught strings of a world shaped not unlike a woman. His right wrist hangs slightly bent, swaying to and fro as he walks, sliding a bow of rain through air cool as a woman's sigh. And the caprice plays inside his head.

Capriccio for solo violin: inspired by the intoxication of freedom, reflecting the lightness of burdens lifted.

Gustavo walks in the Paris rain, from Beaubourg to Luxembourg Gardens, a distance measured not in kilometers but in meters: notes upon a staff. From Beaubourg to Luxembourg Gardens is precisely the length of Gustavo's caprice. And at the end, no applause except the rain on the scattered leaves which he acknowledges with a nod of his head, a modest smile. For every day of rain – and there are many, now that winter has come – there is the opportunity to improve the caprice, change the half notes to quarters, ascending eighths to sixteenths, raise an open G to a sharp, insert a triple stop – all calculated to astound the ears, to make the listener gasp. Revision to perfection. But the length remains the same: from Beaubourg to Luxembourg Gardens.

Gustavo wakes with eyes already fixed on the tall window, hoping for rain. There is rain. It taps on the pane and gathers into rivulets that stream downward and puddle on the stone sill and ease over the edge onto the floor, tapping again – but softer – as it drips onto a sheet of music. He rises, closes the window, picks up the sheet of music and shakes it off. He pauses a moment to stare down at the bed, at the blond hair sprouting across a pillow, the long body wrapped warm in the white sheets, one thin finger jumping in an animated dream. The words come to him without deliberation: *Mi dios, mon dieu, my god, it is good to be alive!*

In the bathroom he stands before the mirror examining his dark perfect features, half hidden now in a coarse beard. He slowly rubs a hand over his face. The whiskers like curled wire scratch the skin of his palm. He frowns. He turns on the faucet and fills the sink with warm water. He opens the medicine cabinet and takes down a new razor.

From Beaubourg to Luxembourg Gardens, the length of Gustavo's caprice.

Mi dios, mon dieu, my god, it is good to be alive!

Gray Paris. A pale wash of thinned ink. Sky, buildings, wet pavement...all gray and bleeding together like ink spilled on a wet page.

Spilled ink... spilled ink... spilled ink...

The gesture repeats itself, recalling something out of his past, a slippery thing he cannot quite put his finger on, yet it prods at something deep inside him. A convulsing of the bowels, an agitation of the soul...

But to hell with the past: *spilled ink.* He was never very fond of art, anyway. Too tangible, too susceptible to dust and time, too dead on the walls of cold echoing rooms. Unlike music. Which is invisible and alive, a shifting thing transported as easily and beautifully as it transports. A thing inside his head that he carries in the silence of the Paris rain. He has not visited the Louvre. He will never visit the Louvre. Not out of defiance toward his past of spilled ink, but out of simple and benign disinterest.

Sunday: The streets especially empty and silent. The resounding heels of his boots a steady cadence beneath the caprice. Do his heels resound? Is their echo really an echo or mimicking footfalls trailing behind him? He abruptly halts. The footfalls continue a moment longer, then halt too. Not his heels resounding, no. The caprice inside his head falters as he slowly looks over his shoulder at the wet gray street behind him, a flash of blue disappearing down a side alley. Heart in his throat, pulse in his ears. A gnawing, gnawing, gnawing...

His bowels convulse.

But he shakes it off, and with it the rain on his back. He glances about, pinpoints the landmarks, gathers his bearings and picks up the caprice precisely where he left off.

Below the Pont Neuf, the Seine lays shivering and gray in the rain, its stench temporarily quelled by the chilled heavy air. At the river's edge, two men in yellow slickers bend over the embankment, hands on knees, peering down at something long and thin and white bobbing in the water. Again, the caprice inside Gustavo's head falters as he pauses on the bridge to watch. One of the men – Gustavo can see now they are policemen – reaches down and grabs hold of the white object. It seems to break apart as the policeman pulls upward, but it is only a naked arm lifted away from a naked body that floats face down in the Seine.

The caprice inside Gustavo's head dies. He presses his hands flat on the cold stone of the bridge and leans forward, squinting through rain.

The policeman drops the arm, heavily, causing the body to bob deeper in the water. He stands, stares at his hand, then repeatedly wipes it against his slicker. The other policeman stands, too. For a long while they remain motionless on the riverbank, gazing down at the naked body, talking quietly among themselves, nodding their heads.

For a long while Gustavo remains motionless too, gazing down at the naked body, longing to see its face, wondering what final verdict it set upon the world before death arrived. He lifts his head and stares out at the gray-bleeding panorama. He raises a hand to rub his beard and flinches upon finding it gone – now only the smooth shaved skin of a face near perfection in its undisguised beauty. He touches his lips wet with rain with fingers wet with rain. He rubs his wet hands over his wet face, through his wet hair. A memory tugs at him, begging to be recognized. A gnawing insistence: *Me, me, me, do you remember?* He ignores it, though his bowels convulse. Then: the unmistakable sensation of being watched.

He quickly glances left, then right: The streets empty and silent.

Cold enters his fingers. Gloom enters his heart. Mozart enters his head: *The Requiem in D Minor: Dies irae.*

Far below, a naked body bobs in the Seine.

Mi dios. Mon dieu. My god. It is good to be alive?

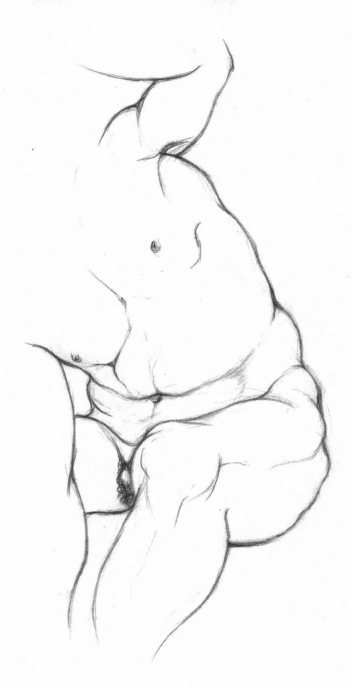

IV. Andante con sordino
What does the body require

— one —

What does the body require? A hundred things. To name a few:

Air: Madeline breathes. The air is cold on her teeth. In Italy or another country there is air, and sometimes it is good air. Here in Italy, in Bagno di Tristezza, it is good. She breathes it. Her body is satisfied.

Water: Madeline drinks. Not from the faucet.

"This water is bad," says Stefano, "demons in the pipes."

At the spring across the road Madeline holds an empty jug beneath the spigot and raises the pump handle. Good water pours out. The water is good because it flows through the hills surrounding this valley, and the rocks beneath the hills filter the water, so it is good. When the jug is full, Madeline bends down and lets the water pour into her mouth. Cold water, and good. She drinks it. Her body is satisfied.

Food: Madeline eats. In the kitchen above the main room of the tower, she boils lentils and onions and carrots and cilantro in a pot on a single propane burner. When the lentils are soft, she turns off the burner and sits in a chair and waits for the lentils to cool. When they have cooled, she takes a big spoon from the cupboard and eats from the pot. Her body is satisfied.

Sleep: Madeline sleeps. There is no clock to tell her when to undress and climb into the tower's big bed. She has no schedule to keep, no deadlines to meet, no one to tell her, "Madeline, it is late. Come to bed, please." When she is tired, she sleeps. Her body is satisfied.

What else?

A hundred things.

For example:

Sex.

"Gustavo, come here!"

"I am practicing, Maddi!"

"You've been practicing for hours. Practice me."

"What?"

"Practice me. Not your violin. Your violin has had enough practice this week. I haven't."

"You never have enough."

"That's not true. I have enough when I have it. And then my body forgets and has to have more. Help my body remember."

"Later."

"Now, Gustavo."

Madeline stepped into the living room and stood naked before Gustavo, her body shaped not unlike a violin.

Gustavo smiled.

Then: Gustavo on Madeline, Gustavo in Madeline.

"Maddi, what would you do if I was not here to help your body remember?"

"Find another man."

"But you love me."

"My heart loves you, my soul loves you, but my body can't tell the difference between one man and the next."

"You are certain of this?"

"Yes."

"Ah. Well. I am here now."

"Yes, you are here now. In abundance."

Dear Gustavo: You are absent now. In abundance.

Clifford Beale was there.

Two weeks after Gustavo walked out and did not come back, Madeline woke with her hand between her thighs. She stepped out of her apartment, walked twenty feet down the hallway and knocked on Clifford's door. He answered. He stood in his boxer shorts and ran his hands through his tousled hair and said, "Madeline." She nodded. He opened the door wide. She walked in. She glanced into his bedroom, at the bed that was rumpled and empty, then turned and stared at Clifford until he asked, "Are you all right?" She shook her head no and pressed the palms of her hands flat against his smooth pale chest. He looked at her hands, then at her face, and understood.

What does the body require?

Lips against lips. Tongue against tongue. Skin against skin. Blood against blood. Groping, clutching, thrusting, contracting, writhing, aching...

This.

With you or without you. This.

The body makes its demands. The demands are satisfied. *This* has nothing to do with love. Nor even hate.

Afterward Clifford lay with his head on Madeline's breast listening to her heart with his left ear and to the aria from Puccini's *Manon Lescaut* with his right. Though the music of Madeline's heart and the music of Puccini's aria were not the same, their words were identical: *Sola, perduta, abbandonata...*

"I would do anything for you, Madeline."

Alone...

"Anything?"

...lost...

"Yes."

...abandoned...

"Then turn off the music."

– two –

The police arrive in the afternoon. Their clean car
gleams on the cold mud road. Their uniforms are clean.
Their shoes are clean. Their faces, clean. The police
captain is short, surly, thick in the middle. He holds a
black woolen scarf in his left hand. From the tower's
high window Madeline squints at the scarf and
absently touches her head.

Topi is the first to greet the policemen. She limps
forward on wobbly legs, tail drooping, head drooping,
mouth hung open in a pitiful expectant grin. Her desire
for affection exceeds the risk of abuse: She stops near
Massimo's shiny black shoes and waits, prepared to
moan or yelp. But he grins with his white white teeth
and gets down on his knees and talks to her softly, and
runs a hand over her bony spine. Clumps of hair float
away in the wind. Her eyes blink in ecstasy. Madeline
cannot hear the mucous rattling in Topi's throat, but
she knows it is rattling. She knows death is never far
off – not from Topi, not from Gustavo, not from
Stefano or Angelina or these somber policemen or
anyone in this winter valley, including herself.

Dear Gustavo: Death is a loiterer waiting to dance.

The police captain scowls at Topi, at Massimo
kneeling on the cold mud, at the hair floating away in
the wind. His round head jerks on his neck as he gestures at the floating hair. Massimo stops grinning and
stands. He looks down at the knees of his uniform
which are no longer clean. He attempts to brush off the
mud, but it remains. The captain nods reproachfully,

shouts, flings his arms wide. The black woolen scarf flies out of his hand and settles onto a puddle of muddy water. He rushes to pick it up as it begins to sink beneath the surface. He snaps it like a whip. Muddy water splatters over him, head to foot. Massimo laughs. The captain glares at him. Massimo turns his back and pretends to study the distant hills. His shoulders shake with silent laughter.

Angelina is next to greet the policemen. She walks through the garden and stands at the wooden gate, gray hair loose, wilder than usual. She repeatedly, blindly, pats it with one hand, but it coils away from her head.

The police captain holds up the black woolen scarf, still dripping with water. Angelina touches it, feels it, listens to the captain as he gestures toward the olive groves along Via Veleno. With a wave of her hand, Angelina indicates the tower where Madeline sits in her high window seat looking down. Both policemen follow Angelina's blind gaze, then turn suddenly as Stefano stumbles out of the wood shed carrying a bottle of Chianti in one hand and a magazine in the other.

Massimo takes the magazine from Stefano and flips through it while Stefano responds to the captain's questions with a posture implying culpability and remorse. Stefano flaps his hands through the air. The Chianti sloshes out of the bottle and onto the shoes of the captain who scowls down at them, then up at Stefano who ducks his head between his shoulders and starts to skulk away. The captain snatches the Chianti from Stefano and pours it out onto the ground while Stefano watches, weeping in dismay.

Massimo looks at the magazine and shakes his head. He pinches the pages between two fingers and turns them around for all to see: a centerfold of a big-busted signorina with legs spread wide. The captain nods appreciatively. Stefano grins and points out the more appealing aspects of the signorina's anatomy. To which Angelina responds by violently slapping the air until her hands hit Stefano across the back of his head. To which Stefano responds by tumbling headfirst onto the ground into a puddle of Chianti and mud.

Madeline's breath exits as fog that whitens across the window, obliterating a small circle of landscape beyond. She exhales again, longer, hotter, until everything, everyone disappears. With the index finger of her right hand, she draws the perfect profile of Gustavo. Beneath it she writes: *Husband.* And beneath that: *Bastard.* And beneath that: *Father.* And beneath that: the perfect profile of a man whom Gustavo resembles. She does not realize she is humming Schubert's *Nachtviolen.*

When Gustavo turned thirty, Madeline threw a small dinner party for him at their apartment. Close friends attended – musicians, artists, writers. And Clifford Beale with his young shy pretty date. And Bernard Allande who came alone but sat next to Clifford's date and flirted with her shamelessly throughout dinner just to watch her blush. Clifford did not seem to mind. He listened cheerfully to the animated conversations around him and every now and then stole glances at Madeline who appeared particularly radiant that evening – perhaps because of the wine, or perhaps because of Gustavo who had kissed her passionately after opening his birthday gift from her: two first class tickets to Rome.

At some point during the evening, after nearly all the wine had been drunk and Chopin's *Nocturne No. 13* played in the background, Bernard Allande shifted his attention from Clifford's date to Clifford, pulling him aside and engaging him in an intense conversation in French which Clifford, although quite drunk, managed with fluid ease. Madeline, who did not speak French, tried to eavesdrop on their conversation. She tried to eavesdrop because Gustavo, who spoke passable French, was eavesdropping, his face somber and tense and fixed.

Suddenly Bernard Allande turned to look at Madeline and Gustavo, and with a thin smile of triumph on his lips announced, *"Tiens!* Such a coincidence! Gustavo Rivera and Madeline Rivera, both abandoned by their fathers at a young and innocent age."

Conversations died. Heads turned, first toward Bernard, then toward Madeline and Gustavo who sat frozen in the moment until Madeline also turned her head toward Gustavo and quietly asked, "Is it true?"

Gustavo's lips tightened. He stared at Bernard without blinking.

Bernard slapped a hand to his cheek and let his jaw drop. "You did not know this, Madeline Rivera?"

Madeline said nothing.

Bernard took a sip of wine and leaned forward across the table, his blond hair falling across his forehead. "Yes," he whispered loud enough so that everyone, if they strained a bit, could hear. "Gustavo's father ran away to Brazil immediately after breaking two ribs of Gustavo's mother. Or was it three?"

Madeline frowned, but it was a pensive frown. Unlike Gustavo's, hostile as he said, *sotto voce:* "Shut up, Bernard."

Bernard did not shut up. "Yes, ribs. I wonder…hmm-m-m. I wonder if perhaps there was the symbolic in his final gesture. Woman made from the rib of man?" Bernard vanished momentarily into some interior realm of speculation, then reappeared with a determined glint in his eyes. "*Alors.* Gustavo's mother was never the same, poor woman. *Pobracita!* And Gustavo, at such a tender age, was never the same, as well. *Sans choix*…without choice he became – how do you say? – the man of the house. Yes, and not only the son, but the father and the husband. The lover, too?"

Gustavo squeezed the napkin in his left hand until his knuckles turned white. Madeline laid her hand on Gustavo's thigh and took comfort in its hardness, its warmth. Clifford stared at his plate, at a bone left upon it, stripped of meat. Although the guests were discomfited by Bernard's soliloquy, they were equally enraptured, unable to turn their ears from Bernard's voice or their eyes from Bernard's handsome but not beautiful face. They assumed he was drunk, though remarkably and provocatively articulate.

Bernard Allande set his elbow on the table and leaned his head lazily upon his hand. "Such a responsibility for one so young! Yes, yes. And how does a child escape such responsibility?" His eyes roamed the dark edges of the room as if to locate the answers hidden there. Two of the dinner guests glanced at the darkness, too.

"How?" Bernard repeated. "Actually, it is quite simple. He, or she," and he looked at Madeline, "escapes into the solitude of art. Music or painting or writing, for example." He fixed his gaze upon the writers seated across the table. "Yes. Into the solitude of art which can be controlled, manipulated, mastered. Which is loyal, dependable, safe. Art will not abandon one as long as one does not abandon art. *C'est vrai?*"

Bernard leaned back in his chair and raised his eyebrows. "And so, *voici!* A violinist and a painter, abandoned by their fathers at such a young age, and now together, here, as adults. Husband and wife! I wonder," he smiled victoriously, "what will be the final consequence of such a union?"

For a long while no one spoke. Then Clifford's young shy pretty date said quietly, in a voice shrill with nervousness and uncertainty, "Maybe they'll grow old together and die happy in each other's arms?"

Everyone looked at her incredulously, including Clifford, including Gustavo, including Madeline who wished to believe her yet knew the stupidity of her words.

Bernard Allande snorted and patted the young woman tragically on the head. "Ah, *cherie!*"

The party ended soon thereafter.

Madeline and Gustavo cleared the table in silence. Gustavo poured leftover wine from one glass into leftover wine from another glass and drank it down. Madeline watched him out of the corner of one eye and asked, "Why didn't you tell me?"

"Tell you what?"

"About your father. About your mother."

"You did not ask."

"I told you about mine."

"I asked."

"But you could have told me then, after I told you. Then would have been the perfect time to tell me."

"It does not matter."

"Yes, it does."

Gustavo slammed the wineglass onto the table, shattering the stem. "No, Madeline! It does not matter! It is the past! I do not live there, not in yesterday! I live only in today! Yesterday is a dead thing! Do you understand? It is dead!"

Madeline stared at Gustavo who stared back for a long silent moment and then picked up a stack of plates and carried them into the kitchen. Madeline followed. She dropped the tableware into the sink where Gustavo stood watching soapy water rise over the dirty dishes. She stared at his perfect profile that was dead, without emotion, and asked, "But why did you tell Bernard Allande about your father?"

"I do not know."

"Of all people, why Bernard?"

Gustavo closed his eyes and sighed wearily. "I do not know and do not ask me again."

She didn't.

– three –

To the right of the tower's south window, opposite the bed, a mirror hangs on the wall. It is an enormous mirror in an enormous gilt frame: nine feet high, nine feet wide. It hangs leaning outward so that the bed is reflected in its entirety when one lies on the bed looking into the mirror. Madeline lies on the bed looking into the mirror. It is an old mirror. Behind the glass the silver is tarnished here, chipped there: black spots like absence reflected, like things vanished and never returned.

Madeline stares at her reflection, at the parts of her body that have not yet vanished. She thinks of the tall policeman, imagines his scent, imagines him in his tight uniform, standing in front of the mirror, slowly undressing, gazing down at her, wanting.

She slips a hand beneath her sweater and slides it over her breasts. They are full and tender. Soon her womb will ache with blood. But now it aches with desire. A desire so acute she can feel her vagina contracting, her cheeks flush hot from the depth of the contractions: The body makes it demands. The demands are precise: Lips against lips, tongue against tongue, skin against skin, blood against blood. Groping, clutching, thrusting, contracting, writhing, aching... This.

She unzips her jeans and pulls them over her hips and slips a hand between her thighs. Her cunt is moist and warm: Her soul may be dead but her body is alive. It requires. This. Precisely this.

Precisely?

A cold winter. Birds fled. Branches of trees knocked in the biting wind. The sky ached with unspent snow. Grass froze hard as glass, shattered beneath footsteps. Inside the yellow bedroom it was warm.

Madeline's body woke before her mind abandoned its dreams. Dreaming, her mind yearned toward some vague consummation of the flesh. Awake, her flesh yearned toward Gustavo who was distant now even in sleep, his body curled like a child's, hugging the edge of the bed as if prepared for swift escape. Madeline's body yearned, stretched itself tight against Gustavo's back. Her hand reached around his waist and searched for his black pubic hair, plunged, found his flaccid cock, cupped it, stroked it, squeezed it until it filled with blood. He moaned. A moan like pain, like sorrow, like the moan before death. Madeline's mind dreamed of Gustavo dying: laid out on the mud bank of some unknown shore, naked and wet and gasping like a dying fish, mythological, the last of its species. A haunting dream. A nightmare. It frightened Madeline's mind awake, and her body jerked against Gustavo's back, her hand contracted, squeezed his cock tight as if it were the ballast preventing her from listing back into sleep.

Gustavo mumbled, "Don't."

"Why not?"

Gustavo did not reply. After a pause Madeline said, "You came home late last night."

Gustavo mumbled, "I had a rehearsal."

"Until two o'clock in the morning?"

Gustavo did not reply. Madeline relaxed her grip on Gustavo's cock, slid her fingers down its hard length, and found his scrotum and gently stroked it.

"Maddi, I cannot."

Madeline rose up on one elbow and leaned over Gustavo's shoulder and peered into his face. His eyes were open, fixed on the door: the closed door beyond which lay a world of freedom, of possibilities. Madeline whispered into his ear, "Come on, Gustavo," and she reached for the white porcelain bell that sat on the night table near Gustavo's head. But Gustavo's hand reached the bell first and picked it up and flung it hard against the door where it shattered into a hundred pieces.

Madeline was still staring at the shards upon the floor, her arm frozen in an incomplete reach, when Gustavo grabbed her wrist and rolled his left shoulder toward her left shoulder so that she fell back on the bed, and he pressed her wrist firmly against her pubis and bent her fingers down between her thighs and frowned at them and said, "I cannot, I cannot, I cannot," and then retreated to the edge of the bed and curled up again like a child, staring at the door beyond which lay a world of freedom and possibilities.

Madeline felt shame, and the shame was red: spreading over her chest, up her neck, through her cheeks. Her eyes red too, and wet with shame. And when the shame had run its red course, it gave way to anger. White anger. She stared at the nape of Gustavo's neck and laid her tender wrist upon her pubis and cleaved her labia and found her clitoris and masturbated while she stared at the nape of Gustavo's neck. She came silently, biting her upper lip, sucking the warm air of the yellow bedroom through her nostrils and exhaling it hotly against the nape of Gustavo's neck where it lifted the black hairs, there, where the black hairs rose and fell.

Gustavo stared at the door and said, "Do you feel better now?"

Madeline stared at the nape of Gustavo's neck and said, "Go to hell."

Madeline's hand falls limp between her thighs. She looks into the enormous mirror at her reflection eaten away by black spots of absence, then looks at the ceiling. Masturbation is not sex. Masturbation is masturbation. A caustic reminder of singleness and isolation.

Dear Gustavo: I have all the reminders I need.

– four –

The chill of the olive picker's death is still on Madeline's fingers. Odd sensation. She did not even know the woman's name.

Dear Gustavo: I did not even know her name. But I know I liked her music. You would have said, Shit. I would have said, Life. You would have said, Then life is shit. Finally, we would have agreed on something.

Via Veleno ends at the highway that passes through the gloomy heart of Bagno di Tristezza. There are no sidewalks here, only a narrow shoulder on either side, and below each shoulder a shallow ditch filled with wet paper and crumpled cellophane and cigarette butts and empty liquor bottles. To walk along the highway is to feel the dangerous wake of each car that passes, is to take one's own life into one's own hands.

Madeline takes her life into her hands. It is weightless, her life. So light, so hollow, as if it does not exist. It does not exist. It is shit. Without Gustavo. With Gustavo. Shit.

She says, "Shit!"

Massimo hears the word, "Shit," hears heels pounding on cold mud. He steps out onto the balcony to watch Madeline pass through the gloomy heart of Bagno di Tristezza. He tries to see what she sees:

Laundry that will never dry hangs on clotheslines, sagging in the damp air. Weeds choke the tiny gardens. Skinny dogs on long chains pace inside the fenced barren lawns. Houses fall deeper into disrepair. And the people absent with their miserable lives that take them into Florence during the day where they work as laborers or sales clerks or waiters. The economy is bad. Tourism is down, retail is down, construction is down, money is hard to come by. At night the people return to their sad homes along the highway of Bagno di Tristezza and drink and argue and sleep and dream of waking in another country, another life. In the morning when they wake in the same country, the same life, they drink coffee with a shot of grappa and dress for work and step out of their sad homes and see a woman dressed all in black passing by, and they whisper, *"La madonna nera,"* and they nod, *"La madonna della morte,"* and they envision themselves dying here in the gloomy heart of Bagno di Tristezza and they want to cry.

Massimo wants to cry. Instead he sighs, "Ah, *sí, sí, sí,*" and looks down between his shiny black shoes where a caterpillar is curled against the cold. He picks it up, breathes on it, waits for it to awaken.

A car speeds down the highway that passes by the sad houses of Bagno di Tristezza. Madeline hears the car behind her, hears its gears shifting to accelerate. Her black shoes crush the dry grass of the highway's shoulder. She watches her shoes move mechanically forward, disconnected from her brain.

The car draws nearer. Madeline's shoes move forward.

Nearer. Forward.

The car roars. Madeline's shoes veer quickly and decidedly left onto the paved highway in front of the speeding car as she closes her eyes, anticipating the impact, the fatal blow.

Massimo gasps.

Tires squeal as the car swerves around her. Its wake whips Madeline's black coat. Its horn blasts long and angry in Madeline's ears, fading as the car swerves back into the right lane and disappears down the highway toward Florence.

There is no impact. No fatal blow.

Massimo exhales.

Madeline opens her eyes and says, "Shit." Stares down at her black shoes that now stand motionless on the gray pavement. Sees something silver to the right of her right shoe. She bends down and picks it up. It is a coin, a lira, almost new. She polishes it against the black wool of her coat sleeve until it shines, then drops it into her pocket and continues walking down the highway.

Money is money.

Madeline did not want to tell Gustavo about the money. She did not want to tell him, but she did.

Her sister said, "Don't tell him about our inheritance."

Madeline asked, "Why not?"

"He's a poor musician and foreign," said Krissy. "Two hundred thousand dollars is a lot of money to a man as poor as Gustavo. You don't know him. You don't know what he's capable of."

Madeline laughed, "I'm not afraid of Gustavo. If anything, he should be afraid of me."

Krissy leaned forward. "What's that supposed to mean?"

Madeline shrugged. "Nothing. I won't tell him about the inheritance. I never intended to."

She did not intend to, but she did.

Gustavo sat playing his violin in a stiff wooden chair,
the only chair in the room, the only room in the
apartment except for a bathroom that was small and old
with crumbling tiles and plumbing that worked
intermittently. The apartment of a poor but beautiful
musician from Chile whom Madeline had met just three
weeks earlier.

Gustavo played his violin while Madeline sat on the
floor and silently wept. Not from the beauty of
Mahler's music – precisely: *Adagietto from Symphony No.
5 in C-sharp minor* – though Mahler's music had a
beauty of its own. No, Madeline wept from the
indescribable beauty of Gustavo: hair, eyes, nose, lips,
neck, shoulders, arms, hands, fingers, chest, stomach,
abdomen, groin, thighs, knees, calves, ankles, feet,
toes…all indescribable in the way they came together
to form a beauty unlike any Madeline had seen.
Abandoned by words, she wept.

Her weeping pleased Gustavo who believed it was
the beauty of Mahler that moved her. He dried her
tears and said, "Ah, yes, I will teach you, Madeline. I
will teach you to love music as I love it – well, almost."

He carried her to his bed and laid her down and made
love to her and she wept again.

Gustavo asked, "But where is the music now?"

Madeline pointed to her heart and sobbed, "Here."

The telephone rang. Gustavo answered it. Madeline
lay pressed against Gustavo's back, listening:

"Yes? Ah, hello! No, not tonight. Saturday? I have
a concert Saturday. Yes, Sunday is possible, but I
cannot stay all the night. No. I cannot. I will not. We
have discussed this before, we will not discuss it again.

Bueno. Yes, okay then. All right then. Sunday. I will bring wine. But I cannot stay, you understand this? Yes, well, so that you understand. Good-bye."

Gustavo hung up and slid an arm beneath Madeline's shoulders and closed his eyes and went to sleep. Madeline held her breath, hoping to quiet the noise of her heart that now played a baleful music.

There were other women. Madeline knew this. Gustavo had told her, "There are others. I do not apologize." And Madeline had said, "I understand," and she had not lied.

Of course there were others. Madeline was not the only one who recognized Gustavo's beauty, nor was she the only one who wished to possess it. But other women could not appreciate the depth of Gustavo's beauty as Madeline appreciated it, could they? Artist, aesthete: born, bred, educated, honed. What Madeline knew that other women did not: Gustavo's beauty was pervasive, a vapor that emanated from a burning core enveloped in exquisite flesh. Filling entire rooms, landscapes, air, and the rooms and landscapes and air transformed, made resplendent, as if uncountable years of dust and ash had been suddenly lifted. To be caught in the vapor of Gustavo's beauty was to be transformed. Madeline was transformed: a shifting of cells, a firing of synapses, a permutation of the soul. Gustavo's alchemical beauty: Madeline turned to gold.

Gustavo slept, emanating vapor. Madeline, golden, absorbed it. She got out of bed and sat in the stiff wooden chair and watched Gustavo sleeping. For three hours she studied him, memorizing each plane and curve and angle and hollow and texture and light and shadow. When Gustavo woke and blinked his eyes against the dawn that silhouetted Madeline awake in the stiff wooden chair, Madeline said, "Gustavo, I have something to tell you."

She did not want to tell him about the money, but she did.

Gustavo stared at her in silence, then shrugged his shoulders. "What does it change? You are you. I am I. Money is..." He shrugged again and pulled her onto the bed and made love to her.

Two weeks later Gustavo moved in with Madeline. In one month they were married.

Dear Gustavo: Money is money. I am me, you are you. Thus a promise is a promise, a betrayal a betrayal.

I am me, you are you. Thus like for like, tit for tat, eye for eye, tooth for tooth, pound for pound, blow for blow, measure for measure.

I am me, you are you. Thus, life is life, death is death.

I am me. Thus.

Money is money.

When Gustavo left, he withdrew $148,901 of Madeline's inheritance.

Dear Gustavo: Why the $1?

The cafe sits at the edge of the highway next to a parking lot where the bus for Florence departs every two hours. There is nothing remarkable about the cafe.

It is small, white and stucco. Inside there is espresso and pastries and bus tickets to Florence, and a woman behind the espresso bar who is perpetually anxious because in Bagno di Tristezza business is never as good as it should be.

Madeline enters. The bell above the door rings a fragile music: familiar.

The woman behind the espresso bar looks up from her magazine and smiles a nervous smile, then spreads her hands flat on the bar as if bracing herself for a difficult task. Madeline mutely points to the espresso machine, then at the biscotti in a jar behind the bar. The woman nods, takes a biscotto from the jar and makes espresso.

The bell above the door rings its familiar fragile music. Madeline starts to turn toward the sound, then remembers she is deaf now. She feels the presence behind her, detects the faint aroma of soap and smoke and something thick and provocative and unnamable that tells her the presence is a man.

The woman glances up from the espresso machine and smiles at the man standing behind Madeline and cheerfully says, *"Giorno!"* and, *"Something-something-something mattino."*

The man laughs – a soft sonorous laugh – and replies, "Ah, *sí, sí, sí."* He begins singing, faintly singing Puccini's *I Pagliacci.* His breath grazes the back of Madeline's neck with a scent of cinnamon. She wants to turn and look at his face, at the face behind the slow sliding melody of a voice that causes something to shift inside her – a throbbing of the breasts, a prolonged spasm between the thighs, a quickening of the blood – but she does not turn. She is deaf. To be deaf when the ears absorb every nuance of sound requires remarkable restraint.

The woman sets the espresso in front of Madeline and waits. Madeline reaches for the worn slip of paper in her pocket – *Io sono sorda. Per favore, me lo scriva* – but the woman already knows the words and pushes the paper away. She writes a sum on a notepad and holds it up to Madeline's face, closely, as if Madeline were blind not deaf. Madeline nods once, then places the lire, coin by coin, on the bar until her pockets are empty. Madeline looks at the woman expectantly, waiting for her to extract the sum from the pile of lire on the bar. The woman looks at the lire, shakes her head, points to the number on the notepad. Madeline searches her pockets again and finds only the coin from alongside the road. She places it on the counter. The woman shakes her head. Madeline wants to say, "Shit," but she is deaf and presumably mute. Her cheeks burn red. She looks at the woman who looks back with less patience than before: Deaf or not, money is money.

Madeline pushes the biscotto away. The woman snatches it, mumbling irritably, just as a hand reaches around Madeline and lays the balance of lire on the bar. Madeline looks at the hand, a thick hand with thick brown fingers jutting from a dark blue coat sleeve trimmed with brass buttons. Now she can turn.

Dear Gustavo: What the body requires, the mind seeks. What the mind seeks, fate supplies. Sometimes this is a good thing.

Massimo stares into the emptiness of Madeline's eyes and is mesmerized, struck dumb. He composes himself. Smiles. Speaks incomprehensible words smooth and sweet and gentle – *legato, dolce, leise.* He removes his cap and slicks back his hair.

Madeline inhales.

It is black hair. His eyes are black. His skin is brown. His teeth are white as paper. He resembles Gustavo.

At the airport in Rome, Madeline handed Clifford a blue envelope and said, "You'll need these."

"What are they?"

"Photographs of Gustavo."

Clifford opened the envelope, took out the photographs and glanced through them: Gustavo pensive, reading a book in lamplight. Gustavo sanguine, leaning against the rough bark of a tree. Gustavo rapt, playing his violin in a stiff wooden chair. Gustavo amused, laughing with Bernard Allande at a post-concert party. Gustavo irritated, picking lint from his shirt cuff. Gustavo doubtful, dancing with Madeline at their wedding reception. Gustavo fascinated, listening to a young female musician backstage at the symphony. Gustavo bored, staring out the window of the yellow bedroom. Gustavo sleeping, sprawled naked on the sheets as if dead.

Clifford smiled, jealousy pinching his eyes. "Gustavo's a handsome guy. The camera doesn't do him justice, does it."

"No," said Madeline. "Justice is my job."

Clifford looked at her and raised two fingers to her cheek and drew an imaginary line down to her mouth. "I'll find him for you, Madeline. I'll make things right."

"No, that's my job, too."

Clifford slowly put the photographs back to the envelope. He looked at his shoes, then at the departing planes. "When you see him again, will you want him again?"

Madeline tilted her head sideways. "As if I ever stopped wanting."

Massimo composes himself, smiles, speaks incomprehensible words smooth and sweet and gentle — *legato, dolce, leise.*

Madeline takes the slip of paper out of her pocket and gives it to the policeman.

Io sono sorda. Per favore, me lo scriva.

He reads it. His black eyebrows briefly arch. His smile wavers. He stares into the emptiness of Madeline's eyes, raises one finger, then takes a small notebook from his pocket and writes:

Voi sei molta bella. Il vostro occhio,
somiglia il cielo tragico.

Madeline studies the words as if their shape will bring their meaning to light, but they remain in darkness. She shakes her head. Massimo nods enthusiastically. She tucks the words into her pocket, then pulls out her passport and opens it and hands it to him. He looks at her photograph, her name, her birthdate, her country. He nods and grins. "Ah! American."

The woman behind the espresso bar glances up in surprise. *"Americana?"*

"Sí! Americana!"

"E sorda?" the woman asks dubiously, frowning now, eyes thin and hard.

Madeline smiles and retrieves her passport. Massimo looks at her black coat and black shoes, at her hair damp with rain, ears red from the cold. *"Sorda?"* he whispers pensively. He watches Madeline drink her espresso in one gulp and take one bite of her biscotto and walk to the door. The bell above it rings fragile and familiar. Madeline looks up at it, pauses, turns to Massimo whose lips are slightly parted as if nearing a kiss. Madeline thumps on her chest and says: "I am... *Io sono... Io sono la madonna nera. Io sono la madonna della morte."*

Madeline and Gustavo sucked in the silence that followed sex in the yellow bedroom where the heat of their bodies and the heat of the summer made the air thick and humid and sweet and seductively pungent.

Gustavo wiped the palm of his hands over the sweat of his chest, then rubbed his sweat over Madeline's breasts slick with oil, rubbed carefully, tenderly as if polishing wood. He traced the long curve from Madeline's left shoulder to her hip, followed the curve with his black eyes, whispered, *"Musica de mi vida,"* and kissed the fine parabola of Madeline's waist and lay his head on her belly and closed his eyes from which tears fell onto Madeline's hot skin and pooled there and ran in a single thin stream down her hip and fell onto the bed.

Madeline combed her fingers through Gustavo's wet black hair, slicking it back, away from his face that was beautiful and brown and gleaming with tears and sweat in the heat of a July afternoon and the aftermath of sex. "Why are you crying, Gustavo?"

"I have nothing to give you."

"Give me yourself."

"I give you myself already."

"That is enough."

Gustavo raised his head and looked at Madeline with eyes full of pleading. "Is it?"

Madeline exits the cafe. The bell above the door rings fragile and familiar.

Shortly after midnight, Gustavo kissed Madeline awake and set a small box upon her belly.

"What's this?" Madeline asked, blinking against the lamplight.

"My gift to you."

Madeline sat up in bed and opened the box. Inside, nestled amid layers of tissue paper, was a white porcelain bell trimmed in gold, very small, very fragile: so thin it was nearly transparent, the blown-glass clapper a blue shadow through the bell's thin walls. Madeline held it like a wild bird in her hands.

"You can ring it!" said Gustavo. He picked it up by its gold stem and gently swayed it to and fro and it rang: a lovely delicate peal. Madeline laughed, "Oh!" and Gustavo set the bell in her hands and said with eyes black and serious, "I give you myself, Madeline Rivera. You ring the bell and I will come to you. I will hear it always. I am a musician, I have very good ears. I will hear it and give my self to you."

Madeline rang the fragile bell.

Gustavo said, "Here I am, Madeline Rivera."

Madeline rang the fragile bell.

Gustavo threw off the blankets and climbed between Madeline's feverish thighs. "I give you my heart, Madeline Rivera."

Madeline rang the fragile bell.

Gustavo unfastened his belt and unzipped his trousers and pulled his briefs below his cock which he maneuvered up Madeline's thigh to the curled red-brown hair to the soft pink flesh beneath, letting it pause there, briefly, pressed hard against the rim of the hollow of her sex. "I give you my body, Madeline Rivera."

Madeline rang the fragile bell.

Gustavo entered her with a moan – Gustavo moaning, Madeline moaning – both of them moaning as they sat face to face on the bed, making love, Gustavo pulling Madeline's hips to his hips, Madeline clutching Gustavo's waist with her thighs, her left hand around his neck, her right hand holding the bell that swayed to and fro as they rocked upon the bed: a lovely delicate peal over and over and over and over...

Outside the café Madeline waits in the cold. A mist falls from the heavy gray sky over Bagno di Tristezza. She shivers but it is not the cold that makes her body shiver, her cheeks flame. She waits, a smile on her lips.

The bell above the door rings fragile and familiar. Massimo steps out of the cafe, looks at Madeline who looks at him and shivers in her black coat. He smiles – a tragic helpless smile – and steps near her and hesitantly fingers the sleeve of her coat and looks into her gray empty eyes and speaks smooth and sweet and gentle – *legato, dolce, leise* – his face drawn in irrelevant apology: *"La madonna nera."*

Madeline nods.

"La madonna della morte."

Madeline nods.

Massimo sighs, black eyes wincing as if from pain. "Ah, *sí, sí, sí.*"

– five –

Beauty: Single blossom among rotting stems. Pale moon in a blackened sky. Clear water over dull stones.

This, too.

For the sake of transformation.

Madeline sits in the front seat of the police car staring at the profile of Massimo who does not take his eyes from the road that runs through the heart of Bagno di Tristezza, yet sees, peripherally, Madeline staring at his profile. He keeps his eyes fixed on the road, jaw firm, lips together, though this is hard to do: breathing through his nostrils, catching the scent of Madeline that pervades the close air of the car, that makes his body want to lean toward her, close up the narrow space between his lap and hers, revealed now inside her black coat open and folded against her thighs: long thighs, muscular, muscles bulging in quiet curves beneath the thin black fabric of her jeans.

Beauty, a relative thing. The ruby red apple does not impress the color-blind. Madeline is not color-blind; she is a painter. She sees the apple is a shocking tantalizing red. Sees with her eyes that are part of her body that desires: *This.*

Transformation: from death to life.

The sudden realization: *Before this moment, I was dead. Now I am half alive.*

"This."

Her voice startles her as much as Massimo who glances at her, then back at the road, his hands gripping the steering wheel tighter as if afraid it will slip out of his control. He says something in Italian.

Madeline, who does not know the question, does not bother with the answer. She slowly reaches toward his face. He jerks away from her hand like a timid animal – a deer, perhaps, simultaneously wild and gentle – and holds his breath as she reaches further, tentatively touching the smooth brown skin of his cheek with the back of two fingers, pressing them there a moment to feel the heat of his skin before trailing them downward across the new stubble, then along his jaw line to his chin where they slide off as she says, *"Che bello."*

He pulls up to the police station, hands trembling as he sets the brake, turns off the ignition, wipes his brow which is damp with sweat, slicks back his hair and looks, finally and pointedly, at Madeline who pierces his black eyes with her gray eyes as she repeats softly, *"Che bello."*

Beauty, a relative thing: The pupils of Madeline's eyes like two crows disappearing into gray skies. His impulsive desire to enter them, to finally know what it means to fly.

The police station is unimposing: a rectangle of cinderblocks covered with stucco painted white, though the white is chipped and dirty, stained a gray-brown near the foundation where rain has poured down from the tiled roofs onto the dirty pavement and splattered up on the white stucco walls.

Inside there is an open room with black metal desks, mismatched chairs, a street map of Bagno di Tristezza tacked to the wall, the highway that runs through the gloomy heart of it drawn in red. Madeline stares at the red highway that ends at the map's left and right edges, dead-ends where the white wall begins as if there were nothing beyond this suburb but blank white death – no streets, no roads, no houses, no shops, no olive groves, no people, no dogs, no laundry, no memory, no pain, no life.

Death: like a white flood, like a flood of pain, like the pain of silence in the ears, the throat, the breast, the groin, the soul into which the music has crawled and died and now lays rotting in the rage of its decay.

Madeline sat in the middle of her studio at three a.m. and stared at the blank white canvas that hung on the wall before her. A violin lullaby ascended and descended: Ravel's *Berceuse sur le nom de Gabriel Fauré*. Ascended again. Descended. Ascended. Madeline stuck a finger in her mouth, tore a piece of flesh from around the nail, and felt nothing. Blood covered her tongue. She pulled the finger out and looked at the blood. A gorgeous violent red. Impossible to mix paint so red.

She stood and walked to the canvas and squeezed her finger until the blood dripped into her palm, pooling there in the cup of her hand: a gorgeous violent pool of red. When the wound was squeezed dry she tore open another, then another until the cup of her palm was full. She slapped the bloody palm against the blank white canvas that was thus no longer blank, no longer wholly white with the explosion of red in the center shaped like a heart that is bleeding, the blood slowly running to the bottom of the canvas and then dripping, once, onto the concrete floor.

The violin lullaby ascended, descended, ascended again.

Madeline walked to the stereo and ejected the cassette and took hold of the tape with her bloody hand and yanked until it unwound in a long thin brown ribbon at her feet. She carried the ribbon to the canvas and stapled it from top to bottom, stretching it over the red-blood bleeding heart in the center, letting the excess hang from the bottom edge of the canvas down to the floor. She picked up a piece of charcoal and wrote *Gustavo Gustavo Gustavo* just below the bleeding heart, and across the bottom edge of the canvas wrote: *What is a life without*

She turned out the lights. She locked the door behind her. She never returned.

Massimo pulls out one of the mismatched chairs – a wooden one, the most comfortable – and gestures for Madeline to sit.

Madeline sits.

Massimo hesitates. His mouth opens as if to speak, but he does not speak. He simply sighs, smiles his sad apologetic smile, and walks toward the small office across the room from which male voices and an occasional laugh spill out. When he enters, the voices and laughter go silent. He speaks – *legato, dolce, leise* – then: the scraping of chairs, a clearing of throats, footsteps. Three faces of policemen peer out through the office doorway, hovering with their curious expressions before being parted from behind by the police captain who pushes through them and walks up to Madeline and puts his hands on his knees and squints into her face and asks slowly, gruffly, *"La madonna nera?"*

Madeline says, "I don't speak Italian."

He snaps his short spine straight, frowns, yells over his shoulder, "Paulo!"

A middle-aged policeman with a round pleasant face and nose like Dante comes forward clutching a black woolen scarf in his hands. Words are exchanged.

Paulo holds the scarf toward Madeline. Clears his throat once, twice, three times. Says, with a thick accent and miserable self-consciousness, "This is your...your...your..." He stares at the scarf in his hands, struggling with language.

"Scarf," says Madeline.

Paulo looks at her gratefully. "Scarf."

"Yes."

"Okay." He nods to the surly police captain who nods back, pulls up a chair, gestures for Paulo to also sit. Paulo sits. The others, including Massimo with his sad irrelevant smile, sit along the room's periphery, as quiet and attentive as polite school children. The police captain pulls a cheap tape recorder from the desk drawer and sets it in front of Madeline. He presses the record button and nods at Paulo who nervously, repeatedly squeezes his left thumb tight inside his left hand and with his right hand rubs the Italian-English dictionary balanced on his right knee.

The interrogation begins.

— six —

— *Did you kill Signora Marcelli?*
— *Who is Signora Marcelli?*
— *She is the woman who is dead, who wore your black scarf on her dead face.*
— *The olive picker.*
— *Olive picker, yes.*
— *No.*
— *No?*
— *I did not kill her.*
— *But why your scarf on her dead face?*
— *To protect her eyes. To hide her eyes from the terror of nothing in the distance that stretches beyond death. No God, no ghosts, no door to the womb. Nothing.*
— *You do not believe in God?*
— *I do not believe in a god who thinks as I think, who needs as I need, who aches as I ache. God help us all if God feels such misery.*
— *If you do not believe, then you can tell to us what is false without...conscience.*
— *Yes, but I will not lie. I have no fear of the truth.*
— *Così. Okay, the truth: At what time you discover Signora Marcelli?*
— *I don't know. Nine, perhaps ten in the morning.*
— *And Signora Marcelli was dead when you discovered she?*
— *Yes, dead. Very dead. Cold.*
— *How much cold?*
— *Cold like the mud of Via Veleno.*
— *And why you were in the olive grove?*
— *I heard no music.*
— *Music?*

— *Signora Marcelli sang every morning... no, hummed. Every morning she hummed while she picked olives from the trees. Her fingers bled. Did you see how bloody her fingers were?*

— *Yes.*

— *Her fingers were still bleeding when I found her. It was as if they had not yet been informed of her death, and so they kept bleeding, curled still as if to pluck one last olive from the tree. And perhaps they did. Perhaps that is what death came disguised as: a perfect fat shining olive that Signora Marcelli plucked with her bleeding fingers from the gnarled tree of life.*

— *Yes, well, okay, but we are not speaking poetry now. (He say that, not I. I only translate for him. I like the poetry and want that you know this.)*

— *Thank you, Paulo. May I call you Paulo?*

— *Oh, yes!* Certo! *So now... You say before about the music?*

— *Every morning I walked past the olive grove and heard Signora Marcelli humming.*

— *Humming is...?*

— *Humming.*

— *Humming... One moment, please. Ah,* certo! *Hum. Hum-ing. Mmmm-mm-mmm-mm-mmm-m-mmmm...*

— *What is that melody?*

— *Ah, it is Puccini! "Vissi d'arte" from the opera,* Tosca.

— *And what does it mean, "Vissi d'arte"?*

— *It means, "I lived for the art."*

— *I see.*

— *"I lived for the art, I lived for the love, I never did harm to a living soul."*

— *Yes.*

— *Is true? You never?*

— *I never.*

— *So!*

— *So.*

— *So, yesterday you walk to the olive grove…?*

— *Yesterday at approximately nine or ten in the morning I came upon the olive grove and paused there on the cold mud road to listen to Signora Marcelli hum, but there was only silence. A dreadful, aching silence. The kind of silence that stabs at the heart, twists the blade deeper, leaves the soul wounded and bleeding, choking on its own blood and therefore capable, the soul capable of…many things, hideous things, I suppose, in order to survive, capable of… You see, Paulo, the soul wants so desperately to survive the silence.*

— *I am sorry. I think maybe I do not understand. This silence…?*

— *I paused on the cold mud road of Via Veleno to listen to the music of Signora Marcelli's humming but I heard only silence, and something inside me grew frightened.*

— *Name this thing that frighten you.*

— *The permanence of silence. The sudden possibility that I might never love music again, never again appreciate its beauty and thus never own it. That the silence would deepen inside me and take root in my soul like a poisonous weed and strangle my love of beautiful things, strangle love too – yes, kill it, and consequently kill me, for that is all I have, really. My love of beautiful things.*

— *Here. Take please my* fazzoletto *for to dry your tears.*

— *I'm not crying.*

— *Your eyes are wet.*

— *It's the light. My eyes are sensitive to fluorescent lights, their vibrations, their humming. Their humming reminds me of –*

— *Signora Marcelli?*

— *No, something else. Something... unpleasant. Please, let's continue.*

— *You are certain you have not sadness?*

— *For godsake, Paulo, what has sadness to do with anything – even death?*

— Calmarsi, per favore! *Your angry is not necessary, Signorina, and for what reason this?*

— *I'm not angry. See? I'm smiling. I smile.*

— *Okay.* Bene. So. *You hear no music and you fear silence and this other things – weeds and strangle of beauty, et cetera – and maybe also you fear the death of Signora Marcelli?*

— *Maybe. Her death, or mine, or my husband's.*

— *You are married?*

— *Yes. No.*

— *Which is? Yes or no?*

— *My husband left me for another woman.*

— *Ah, so you are alone now.*

— *Yes.*

— *Your husband, he is in America?*

— *No. He is in Europe. Italy, perhaps. Perhaps France. Perhaps Spain. Perhaps Portugal. Perhaps Germany.*

— *You come here to find your husband or to forget him?*

— *Yes.*

— *Yes, which?*

— *Yes.*

— *Okay, okay, your lost husband is not about the death of Signora Marcelli.*

— *No, but perhaps the death of Signora Marcelli is about my lost husband.*

— *Explain, please.*

— *No.*

— *No?*

— *No.*

— Cosí. *We continue with before. You stop on the Via Veleno and you hear silence and you think, "Some thing is not okay. Some thing is bad."*

— *That's right.*

— *And you walk in the olive grove and you discover...? What you discover?*

— *Signora Marcelli dead on the ground, her eyes open, her legs twisted beneath her like a ragdoll's, her right hand curled as if to pluck... She fell from the ladder, I suppose. Or the ladder fell beneath her. In any event, she died.*

— *A accident.*

— *Yes.*

— *Why you think a accident?*

— *Why would someone want to kill a poor olive picker?*

— *Why would someone want to kill any person is the question we ask every day. The answers, so much time the same: for money, for angry, for hate –*

— *For love.*

— *Yes,* certo! *For love, also! Maybe the most worse murder, the most tragic. First you have love and then – like that! – you have the murder.* Tragico!

— *Yes, but sometimes necessary.*

— *What is this you say?*

— *Nothing. Signora Marcelli's death was an accident.*

— *Yes, okay, maybe at the final she die because her heart stop, but –*

— *A broken heart. Of course.*

— *Maybe, but...*

— *But what? What is he implying, Paulo?*

— *You must understand, Signora, the people who live in Bagno di Tristezza, they are very...* superstizioso.

— *Superstitious.*

— *Yes, thank you. Superstitious. They believe exist God, they believe exist Satan, they believe exist also death in the form of a woman who is thin and pale, with eyes gray and empty of life, who never say nothing, who is silence. And on her back is a black coat, and on her feet the black shoes, and on her head a black scarf – until, of course, she put this scarf over the eyes of a dead olive picker.*

— La madonna nera.

— Sí, *yes.*

— La madonna della morte.

— *Yes. And these people of Bagno di Tristezza, they believe death walk up and down Via Veleno disguised like this woman melancholic, this woman hungry for to kill.*

— *I've killed no one yet.*

— *Yet?*

— *I've killed no one.*

— *Okay, but any way there is death in Bagno di Tristezza. In one month past, there is Signora Marcelli dead, and Tatiana Roberto dead, and Signor Blanco dead, and the son of Mario Trudento dead, and Signorina Flanco have a baby born dead, and oh, yes, there is one goat – not old, not before sick – it is dead, and five chickens dead one night the same time, and three olive trees of Giovianni Malosa dead like that all at once, and...Why you laugh? You think this is some...some...coincidence?*

— *I walk up and down Via Veleno and things die. You believe this?*

— *No, not me, not we here. Our work is to discover the truth from the facts. But the people of Bagno di Tristezza, they are...oh, how do you say again?*

— *Superstitious.*

— *Yes, that. Many are poor. They have the bad luck. They want, they need that their bad luck have a face, and you are a stranger who speak no word to no person ever –* como sorda, sí? *– and so they put your face on their bad luck.*

— *Hm.*

— *They say your heart is black, Madeline Rivera. They say your heart is empty and black. They say your heart need to kill to stop from to fall into itself. They say –*

— *The heart needs, the soul wants, the body desires, the heart needs, the soul wants, the body desires...*

— Scusi? *Signora?*

— *...the heart needs, the soul wants, the...*

— *This is what they say, not we here. The people of Bagno di Tristezza are only super...superstitious.*

— *...body desires, the heart needs...*

— *Of course, there is no evidence of their words.*

— *...the soul wants, the body desires.*

— *Signora Rivera? You are sick?*

— *What is his name?*

— *Who?*

— *The lieutenant there. The tall one, the young one, the one who is nearly beautiful.*

— *His name is Massimo.*

— *Massimo what?*

— *Massimo Benevento.*

— *Perfect. A perfect name for a perfect man nearly beautiful. I want him.*

— Scusi?

— *I want Massimo to take me back to Villa Ferramo. We are finished, correct?*

— *Yes, okay, we finish the questions maybe, but...*

— *But what? Either you lock me up or you let me go. And if you lock me up you must have evidence that I have committed a crime. Do you have evidence?*

— *No, we have no evidence.*

— *That's right, you have none. I am bored with this interrogation. Massimo,* per favore? *Massimo with the black eyes, the black hair, the lips soft and wet.*

— *But, Signora!*

— *What is the problem, Paulo?*

— *You are married still!*

— *Come here. Lean closer, Paulo...closer...and listen to me: My husband is lost in Europe. My body requires.*

— *Requires?*

— *Yes, requires. This...*

— *Oh, oh!* Capisco! *But I think I will not translate that!*

— *Suit yourself.*

V. Scherzo for string quartet
A man this beautiful

A Paris day, wet-veiled and aloof. Music amid silence.

But a Paris night descends like a black-winged oily-winged bird of prey screeching its one hideous note, feeding on the living and picking flesh from the bones of the near dead. The difference between day and night as different as night and day.

In a small dim-lit back room of an expensive restaurant – expensive because it has back rooms, has a maitre'd who for a fee will lead patrons to these back rooms, and who for a fee will guard the privacy of patrons entertaining themselves without discretion in these back rooms until the wee hours of the morning, and who for a fee will never speak of what he has heard patrons saying seen patrons doing in these back rooms cluttered with food and wine and smoke and more often than not body fluids to be mopped up scrubbed away after the night and patrons have gone – here, in a back room, Gustavo smokes a cigar and drinks brandy and stares up at the ceiling which is a large unblemished mirror nine feet by nine feet, the precise dimensions of the room, and watches from a finite distance – the distance between his black eyes and his black eyes reflected – watches the head of a young female violinist bob slowly up and down, up and down on his lap and is pleased, lighthearted, drunk

with satisfaction and brandy because he can simultaneously enjoy felatio and dissect the philosophical conversation of the two patrons seated across the table
from him:

*...descending like a black-winged oily-winged bird of prey
screeching its one hideous note, feeding on the living, picking
flesh from the bones of the near dead...*

"But, really, we all are the near dead, are we not?"
"Not I. I am unmistakably alive. Taste my living
flesh."
"Ah, yes. It is delicious, to be sure. To be sure, and
yet. We cannot move backward into the past, cannot
return to the womb. We move forward, forward. And
it is always death we are moving toward, is it not? Is it
not? Is it not? Is it... Spread your legs for me, *cherie*.
That's right. Yes. Just like that."
The young violinist whose head bobs up and down and
up and down on Gustavo's lap pauses to look up at
Gustavo's face and thinks a thought she is too drunk to
complete but which persists nevertheless: *A man this
beautiful...a man this beautiful...a man this beautiful...*

Gustavo prefers to watch himself fucking a woman
rather than watch the woman he is fucking. Thus in
Paris (a city of freedom and possibilities) there is
always a mirror somewhere in the room, or else there is
no fucking.

A man this beautiful...

recalls now a woman who lived in the apartment
building next to theirs, whose kitchen window was

directly opposite their kitchen window – both windows tall, stretching floor to ceiling. This woman was not particularly pretty – plain of face and hair – but she was young and had large breasts, and in summer when it was hot she would sit at her small kitchen table wearing only a bra and panties, reading a fashion magazine and wiping the perspiration from between her large breasts with the back of her left hand. On hot evenings after sunset he would stroll into the kitchen wearing nothing but a towel and walk up behind his wife and pull back her hair and kiss her neck and lick her ears until she moaned and tilted her head one way or the other, left or right, and closed her eyes. And he would take her then, from behind: dropping his towel, pressing his wife low over the counter where the ingredients for dinner sat waiting to be combined and spoiling in the heat, making certain his profile faced the window across from which the young unpretty woman sat in her bra and panties pretending to read her magazine but watching – indeed, unable to look away from – his beautiful buttocks flexing as he entered his wife, his beautiful legs bent at the knees and remarkably strong with each muscle defined by his desire, his beautiful shoulders pulled straight and then occasionally curling forward to exemplify the wide brown intensity of his back, his beautiful arms sliding up his wife's spine and under her arms to cup her breasts like fruit not so tender they will bruise at the slightest touch – that delicate balance between bruising and not bruising, pain and pleasure – the young unpretty woman perspiring in the summer heat and watching, unable to look away from a man that beautiful...

remembers as he looks at himself in the tall wide heavy gilt-framed mirror that hangs on the wall of his Paris dining room reflecting the mahogany table and himself fucking a lovely young flutist. Unfortunately, it is not quite enough to imagine the awe of a plain young woman who lived in another country a lifetime ago, so he grabs a handful of the flutist's blue-black hair and pulls her head sharply to the left so that she faces the mirror in which her own image is being fucked from behind by a beautiful musician who softly hums Lalo's *Symphonie Espagnole* as he fucks, pausing his humming only to urgently whisper in Spanish, "Am I beautiful to you? Am I a beautiful god?" But the flutist is Korean and does not comprehend Spanish, and in the silence of her incomprehension he closes his eyes and does not see – yet is not surprised by – the hand of the man who reaches out to cup his damp testicles and say in bastardized French, in a tone that could be construed as either sincere or snide, "Ah, beautiful, of course, like a beautiful fucking god of narcissism."

And then a Paris dawn, shrouded and naive. The apartment disheveled: half-empty glasses and cigar butts and clothing and shoes and the soft-breathing bodies of the near dead.

A man this beautiful...

is cursed by the insomnia caused by a nagging memory like a prodding finger interrupting even his deepest sleep: *Me, me, me, do you remember?*

And so he goes to the window that overlooks the street and throws it open and leans out over the sill into the rain already falling like a damp veil upon the whole city, living and dead, falls upon the near dead too, upon his slick black hair and black lashes and black shadow of a new beard. He closes his eyes and inhales. When he opens his eyes he sees a blue-coated figure below huddled in a doorway, hands buried in the pockets of the blue coat, face lost among the shadows – except for the glow of a cigarette stuck between what must be lips, a cigarette glowing red and hot with each long slow inhalation, until one hand comes out of one blue pocket and plucks the cigarette from what must be lips and flicks the cigarette into the street where it flares and spits before drowning in rain.

And he – a man this beautiful – feels the chill of that gesture and the rain and his nearing death, and responds with vertiginous waves of dread and nausea.

And the blue-coated figure steps out of the doorway into the fast-rising dawn and glances up from under a blue baseball cap, glances up at the window where Gustavo dreads, glances up only once and only briefly – yet long enough for the fleeting familiarity of the glance to cause Gustavo's dread to twist and writhe inside his bowels like a beheaded snake – glances up before quickly glancing down at the wet pavement, the wet black boots on feet that hurry away from the window flung wide overhead, and down the street of this wet-veiled aloof city rising now in a perpetually gray light, heels resounding on the pavement: *heel-toe, heel-toe, heel-toe…*

A man this beautiful… this beautiful… this beautiful…

The young violinist starts awake.

…will die, too.

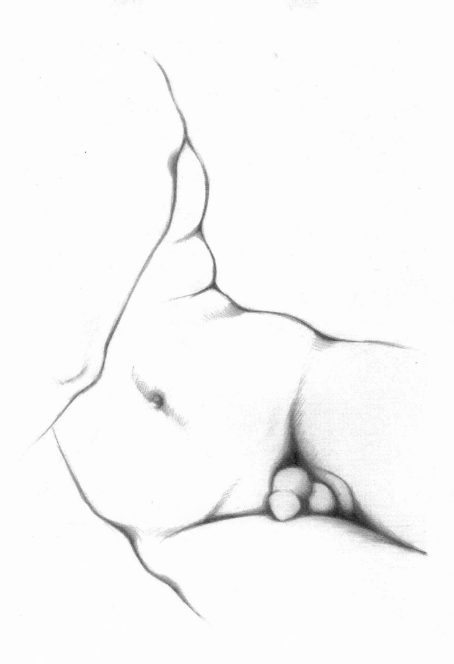

VI. Adagietto Agitato
What is the shape of waiting

– one –

A place resigns itself to the immutable distance of spring, its winter roads hard as bone. There are no pauses in time; time does not stop. Nor will it change its pace, upon request or independently. It moves. Never mind that it is all illusion, that it is really the inventors of clocks who are moving: toward spring, toward sunrise, toward sleep, toward death.

Having never wished to exist, time holds steady out of vengeance.

Bagno di Tristezza. December 12.

In the lowest part of the valley, in a small house nestled among the oaks and pines, smoke curling from its chimney, an old man who will die tomorrow of natural causes and with a slight but unmistakable smile on his lips – *At last, at last!* – sits alone in his library in a chair beside a lamp beside a fire, listening to *La Boheme* on an old record player, thumbing through a book of poems he once understood but now confound him. Now he sees only words, lines on a page, pages of black ink. He shakes his head and sighs. Closes the book. Closes his eyes. Thinks: *If, in this universe of words, meanings have shape, then what is the shape of waiting?*

Ask Stefano and he will belch: *The shape of waiting is a bottle of Chianti, a liver swelled, a wife with useless eyes.*

Ask Stefano's wife and she will groan: *The shape of waiting is the balance of night, dust on the sill, names for the never-born, ache and bruise.*

Ask Madeline and she will spit: *The shape of waiting is black heels on blood-red tiles, and music slain in the heart, and a cock tight inside a fist: blue veins, throbbing pulse, semen rising, the rash and itch of desire.*

Massimo sweats inside the jacket of his police uniform inside his police car whose windows sweat from the heat of his breathing and the heat of Madeline's body crouched between his knees gripping his cock like a weapon, like a club, like a final threat as she licks a single drop of pre-ejaculation oozing from the tip, then licks again the now clean pink-red skin and glances up at Massimo – who resembles Gustavo especially now, now with his eyes half closed and his lips gaping and wet. She smiles at his low shuddering moans, his breathing like sighing, his quiet implacable beseeching of all that is holy: God, Virgin Mary, Jesus, Saint Michael. Smiles and whispers, "Music like a scream," and narrows her eyes as she tightens her grip and opens her mouth and lowers it over Massimo's cock without touching it, only her hot breath touching it, and then pauses, hovering, teeth bared and close.

Waiting shaped like teeth.

In another country Madeline lay up to her eyes in a white bath of warm water growing cold. Between her knees spread wide against the sides of the tub the water lay flat, unrippled, without event or color. When she squinted, allowed her vision to falter, the water's surface appeared to stretch forever into a distance of pure whiteness, emptiness, nothingness: a vision she foresaw as life without a soul, soul-less but with a heart that grieves, bleeds, rages. She drew her knees together and exhaled underwater and sat up and looked at Gustavo who stood at the sink brushing his teeth. Gustavo naked, beautiful, absorbed in his reflection and in a scene that extended beyond his reflection, shifting against the backdrop of Bruch's *Adagio from Violin Concerto No. 1.* A scene animated, erotic, perhaps dangerous.

"Do you believe in the soul?" Madeline asked.

Gustavo spit a mouthful of toothpaste and saliva into the sink. "The soul?"

"Yes, the soul, the spirit."

"Ah. *Espiritu. Alma.*"

"Do you believe?"

He rinsed his mouth with water and spit again. "Sure. I must to believe."

"Why must you?"

"That is where the music is born, where the art is born, in *el alma.* Not in the head, not in the hands, not in the mouth, not in – "

"The cock?"

Gustavo grinned. "Well, maybe some of the music is born here," and he wrapped his fingers around his cock already swelling with blood.

Madeline reached between Gustavo's thighs and grabbed his buttocks and drew him toward her so that his groin was level with her mouth that was slightly agape, teeth almost visible. She brushed her lower lip against his fast-receding foreskin.

Gustavo closed his eyes and said, "Yes, music like a sigh, like a moan, like a whisper –"

"Like a scream?" suggested Madeline, lightly scraping her teeth against the head of his cock.

Gustavo's eyes flashed open, his cock recoiled. He took one step backward, away from Madeline's teeth. "No," he frowned. "Why a scream, why?"

Madeline shrugged. "Not all music is pleasant, Gustavo. I mean, what voice – good or bad, sweet or bitter – is not music?"

Gustavo stared at Madeline a long while before answering: "The silent voice."

"Ah," said Madeline.

Gustavo flossed his teeth. So white, his teeth. Whiter than the porcelain tub upon which Madeline now lay her head in order to stare up at Gustavo's white, white teeth.

Waiting shaped like white, white teeth.

Massimo winces, sucks air between his clenched white teeth, and Madeline – teeth poised, tongue darting – considers how difficult it is to discern between the face of pleasure and the face of pain.

Massimo, in pleasure, feels the heat of Madeline's breath, her hair like bird wings fluttering against his thighs, her fist tight around his cock, and then – what is it? He will never be certain of the sensation, for at the precise moment his brain detects a tacit veering from pleasure toward pain, he rolls his head to the side, toward the sweating window, and sees one green melancholy eye peering at him through a wide clear rivulet racing down the glass.

Massimo's cry like a child's gasp, *"Mi dio!"* as he clasps Madeline's head between his big hands and lifts it up – her teeth scraping, lightly scraping the head of his cock already going soft – and holds her head before him like a ball he is about to toss, or drop, or clutch to his chest, unable to decide which, wanting to do everything at once and so frozen in the moment which is nevertheless passing into another moment. Though he knows that in reality it is he and Madeline and the owner of the green melancholy eye who are passing into yet another moment that in its vengeful stubbornness will neither slow nor look back at the ruination it has wreaked.

"What?" Madeline asks. *"Che cosa?"*

"Mi dispiace, però c'é un uomo..."

"I don't understand. *Non capisco."*

Massimo rotates Madeline's head toward the window and slowly repeats, *"C'é un uomo."*

Madeline rises from between Massimo's naked thighs and wipes the sweat from the window and presses her face close to the glass to look out at the old man who stares back at her, into Madeline's empty gray eyes, emptier than the winter sky which now hangs thick and low with the chilled white fog skulking into the valley before dusk, and the old man is at first horrified, then surprised, then relieved, then grateful: his face easing into a toothless grin as he slowly clasps his hands beneath his chin and lifts his eyes toward heaven and says, silently through the sweaty glass, fog like shifting ice: *"Grazie a Dio! Finalmente! La madonna nera! La madonna della morte!"*

"And speaking of death –" began Bernard Allande.

"Who was speaking of death?" asked Madeline.

"– did you know that a person's true attitude toward death is revealed during the moment of orgasm?"

"Really," asked Clifford. "How so?"

"The orgasm is the lovely death we allow ourselves," Bernard glanced at Gustavo and grinned. "Some, of course, allow themselves more frequently than others."

Gustavo quickly stood and left the room.

Madeline followed him with her eyes but did not follow him with her body because her mind wished to hear what Bernard had to say.

"So," he continued, "one cannot make orgasm without releasing one's hands from the neck of life – if only for a moment, releasing. And so, when we remove our hands from life's neck, when we have our little death, it is only practice for the big death, *oui? Oui.*"

"Practice is practice," said Madeline, "not revelation."

"That's right," said Clifford. "You haven't explained how–"

"Yes, *how*, Monsieur Allande?" Gustavo asked, eyes narrowed, leaning now against the doorframe, not really seeking an answer.

Bernard dragged deeply on his cigarette and winked at Gustavo. "What is it you do exactly when you make orgasm, Señor Rivera? What words do you cry? What expressions do you give? Possibly, are they words and expressions of dread? Does your body tremble – not from pleasure but from fear?" He turned to Clifford. "And you, Monsieur Beale, do you call upon God, beg for His mercy? Or curse Him, and curse yourself? Do you groan as if in pain? Scream as if in terror? Sing as if performing your swan song? Do you cry, *Yes, yes, yes!* as if giving death permission to finally take you?"

Clifford pondered Bernard's question, then replied with an earnestness that caused Gustavo to stifle a laugh. "I say god. No, I say God! Only once. Like an affirmation."

"Ah, a true believer," said Bernard, throwing a hand over his heart. "How very antique!" Then Bernard looked at Madeline and turned up one corner of his mouth, waiting to see if she would volunteer information – impressed, it seemed, that she did not – and so sighing contentedly before asserting: "I imagine, Madeline Rivera, that you weep when you make orgasm. When your blood changes its course, flows back to your feet and head, then your heart is full of so much pleasure – a woman as demanding as you having experienced so few truly satisfying pleasures in life... Yes, yes, full of so much erotic pleasure that you weep from gratitude. And when the tears reach your lips, Madeline Rivera, you lick them away with your tongue, and the salt reminds you of the womb to which you long to return."

Clifford's cheeks burned red as he stole a glance at Madeline whom he imagined now writhing naked upon his lap and weeping. And Madeline stared at Gustavo who stared back at her and blinked once, then scowled at Bernard Allande who took another long drag on his cigarette, started to tamp it out, changed his mind, said, "Ah, yes. I imagine, Madeline Rivera, you weep and then lick away the tears – you who are perpetually thirsty for death."

Inside the sweaty police car: Massimo humming as he enters Madeline again, this time from behind, and Madeline wondering as she licks the salt of her tears.

"And what do you do the moment of orgasm, Bernard?" Madeline asked.

"Oh yes, tell us, *please*," said Gustavo sarcastically. "We are all *dying* to know."

Bernard grinned at Gustavo, then at Clifford, then sobered as he let his eyes fall upon Madeline, fall deeply into Madeline's gray eyes that were not yet empty. He said: "I laugh, of course."

Stefano laughs. He peers through the broken window of the wood shed and laughs, "*La madonna della morte!*"

Madeline pauses on the cold mud road of Via Veleno, clenches the muscles of her vagina, and therefore is able to recall the precise shape and size of Massimo's cock. She smiles.

"*Sí, sí*, is you!" cries Stefano. He disappears from the shed's window and reappears at its door. "You can not to kill me, Signora Rivera, so you send your *cospiratore* to kill me."

"My what?"

"*Cospiratore! Cospiratore!* The one who help you to kill. I know the *schema*. Your *assassina*, she put the pietà in my garden – *o mio bello giardino!* – and the pietà put the poison in my vegetables each time we have rain, and so I eat and die slow and no one – not the *polizia*, not the people who live along Via Veleno, not even, I think, God – no one, no one think it is you who kill me, you and your secret *cospiratore*. But *I* think. *I* know, *la madonna della morte!*" He clutches the neck of

125

his filthy shirt and wails, "I die slow, Signora Rivera, slow, slow, slow!"

Madeline looks at Stefano without compassion, without pity or loathing, without interest at all except to note that Stefano's old gray flesh seems to have shrunk tighter around his skull, tighter around his arthritic knuckles – his ears and bones thus appear to have grown – and his shoulders that barely hold up his head, let alone the world, are more heavily stooped, bent like the olive trees in this cold valley, and the whites of his eyes not white at all but yellow like his teeth, like his fingernails, like the saliva that oozes down his chin and onto his shirt already stained with Chianti and oil and tomato sauce and something brown and vile.

It's true, Madeline thinks, *Stefano is dying.* Yet it is not pointless conspiracy that wastes him so slowly but his own stubborn refusal to die. Stefano has outlived his careless life and so believes he now has a right to it.

"You know nothing," Madeline says and continues walking toward the villa.

Stefano screams after her, "Your *cospiratore*, she is Angelina, yes?"

Madeline does not respond.

"Angelina is she, yes? Your assistant to kill me, yes? YES!?"

Madeline does not respond.

Stefano stumbles after her, staggering on the cold mud, falling once, getting up, falling again, crawling finally on his hands and knees until he reaches Madeline who turns around in time to see him lurch toward her, fling his scrawny arms around her thighs and bury his sodden face in the lap of her black coat, weeping, "Forgive me, forgive me, forgive me..."

Madeline stares down at him. "For what?"

"For to want to live."

Madeline looks out at the silver-green valley of olive groves, at the sky sliding from one shade of gray into another deeper shade, breaking open just above the horizon to reveal a handful of early stars. She listens. Except for Stefano's sobbing and the ceaseless humming wind (no longer resembling music, resembling nothing but itself; only wind, just as it is) there is silence, and yet...

Madeline sniffs her hair that smells like Massimo, like the wet bark of oaks, moss warm in the sun, and stares at the low-slung stars and hears, she believes, someone playing Mozart's *Adagio from Violin Concerto No. 3* somewhere just beyond the furthermost hills. Miles away, perhaps. Perhaps in another country.

— two —

Paris, France
December 1

Dearest delicious Madeline:

Today I went to the Louvre because it was cold outside and I was tired of walking in the damned cold and tired of standing in the cold and tired of waiting in the cold. I stood in front of your favorite painting, *Death of Sardanapalus,* by Delacroix, and I almost cried.

Okay, I did cry. And I wanted to sit down on the floor and cry harder, but instead I got angry.

Why is King Sardanapalus so calm, so fucking arrogant, while he reclines on his big red bed and watches his slaves kill every-thing he loves — his women, his horses? He's going to die, right? His enemies have de-feated his army and they're on their way to kill him, so he's taking everything he loves with him into death, right?

Madeline, my sweetness, why do you love this painting? It's true the reds are pure, "like blood," you said, "like passion." But I kept asking myself as I stood there crying, Which am I? The slave who drags the horse to slaughter? Or the one begging for mercy?

Okay, I've had a lot to drink. A bottle of wine for lunch and I just finished off another. It's that I miss you more than you can know.

Do you know at least that you can't
know how much I miss you?

Cliff

A cold so deep even the earth groans.

Madeline pauses beneath the rotting pergola, her
white breath like a phantom appearing and
disappearing in the winter night. She loosens her grip
on the sack of coal that falls backward onto the other
sacks with a sound like the scuttling of tiny mammals.
There in the cold dark she holds her white breath and
listens: Dry weeds crackle in the wind, branches creak
and snap. Somewhere on the north hills a rabbit falls
prey to a night beast and squeals, then falls silent.

And the earth groans.

It is a groan Madeline has heard before.

After the car skidded on a patch of ice and then slid
off the road into a ditch and then died there in the
thick dry winter bracken and would not start again, the
three of them – Madeline, Gustavo, Bernard Allande –
walked single-file, detached, solemn along the deserted
blacktop toward the home of the symphony conductor
a mile and a half away. There was no moon. But the
sky was clear: myriad stars lit the road, and the empty
pastures alongside the road, and the pale face of
Madeline who walked upon the road behind Gustavo
and in front of Bernard Allande, staring at the white
line that marked the road's edge and the path of her
feet, listening as Bernard lamented over and over
again, "My hands, my hands, my hands," until Gustavo
said with finality, "Put your fucking hands inside your

fucking pockets and stop crying," and then under his breath, *"Infante!"*

Bernard stopped crying.

The three walked in silence.

The earth groaned.

Madeline was not certain of what she heard or from which direction came the sound. She cocked first her left ear then her right toward the wide empty pastures beside the road.

Bernard snorted, "If only Gustavo knew how to drive his automobile as expertly as he plays his violin."

Madeline strained toward the groaning.

"Ah, but wait!" Bernard continued. "If that were the *situation actuelle*, then we would be dead now, yes, and bleeding on this black road of ice."

Gustavo wheeled around. "So now you insult my talent?"

"Talent!" Bernard laughed. "You, *mon cher*, have no talent but to smile in such a way as to make women – and what, men also? – spread for you their thighs warm and soft like fresh baked bread. Do you know this is true, Madeline Rivera, do you know?"

Madeline stared out at the pastures gray in the starlight and said, "Be quiet."

Gustavo leaned his head toward Bernard's, so closely that the clouds of their breathing became entangled, indistinguishable, one from the other. Gustavo said, "And you, my friend growing old – what? Your hands, they begin to curl like dead leaves, so how much time more will you play?"

"I, Bernard Allande," said Bernard Allande, *"virtuoso du violoncelle*, have warmed the hearts of all the world's stages! And you, Gustavo Rivera, have not and will never, never, never – "

Madeline stomped her feet. "Shut up!"

Gustavo and Bernard shut up. Steam rose from their brows.

"Listen," said Madeline, "listen *there*." And she pointed with her whole hand, fingers splayed, toward the pastures gray in the starlight and the far horizon made black by dense stands of elm trees.

Gustavo and Bernard looked at where Madeline pointed, which seemed at everything and nothing all at once, at a place wide and narrow and near and distant. There was no wind, no water, no animals hunting in the night. There was silence. A cold aching silence. The silence of the deadest night of winter. In fact, silence like death falling heavy around the ears of them all, burying them alive, an interment causing the body's music to rise up in their ears: heartbeat, breath, teeth-grate, swallow, churn, twitch, flex... Gustavo shifted uncomfortably within the silence. Bernard gave a little cough and looked at his hands.

Then the earth groaned.

Madeline turned, grinning triumphantly. "Did you hear it?"

Gustavo and Bernard nodded, staring out at the frozen land.

"What do you think it is?" asked Madeline.

"Some animal," said Gustavo.

"No," said Bernard. "It moves wide. Listen."

And indeed, the groaning shifted from left to right, front to back – rippling low, not high like an echo.

Gustavo said, "It is *la terra*. The earth, it freeze and so there is noise."

"Not noise," said Madeline, "music."

Gustavo said, "Shit."

Bernard stared out at the black horizon and said, "Ah, yes! The requiem of winter."

Gustavo and Madeline looked at Bernard who stepped to the edge of the road, onto the gravel of the shoulder, and glanced down at his polished shoes which he took a moment to slowly wipe with the cuff of his jacket. Then he calmly looked up and out at the gray expanse of countryside that could have been anywhere but was not: rather, was there on that night in another country, a lifetime ago.

"They speak of this in the north of Europe," he said. "Deutschland? Finlandia? Suisse? I cannot remember. But, they say on the night when all things die, when no life is left inside the earth, before the first growings of *le printemps*, of spring, the land sings a requiem for the dead, a lamentation for all that dies inside her. It is a rare thing to hear it. Yes, quite rare. And they also say – listen carefully, Gustavo and Madeline Rivera – they also say that the rare souls who hear this winter requiem shall soon also suffer a kind of death. Suffer a complete dying of their old life, so that a new life can begin to grow. A happy new life, or a sad new life, who can say which?"

Gustavo and Madeline stared intently at Bernard Allande – who continued to stare at the horizon, a faint smile on his lips – then they stared at each other: Gustavo at Madeline, Madeline at Gustavo, her gray eyes searching Gustavo's black eyes and finding nothing really, only the slightest shifting as if something had just passed behind her.

Her desire, then: to shift with Gustavo's eyes, to give her eyes a moment more to ask… But what would she ask?

Gustavo glanced down at the road, then at the black horizon. "What shit!"

"It is true!" smiled Bernard Allande.

"It is invention," said Gustavo.

Bernard reached out and laid his bent fingers against Gustavo's cold cheek and said, "Perhaps." Then he stroked his bent fingers over Madeline's hair and said, "Perhaps not."

Dear Gustavo: Perhaps not.

Immediately after they arrived at the conductor's house, after the conductor's young and lovely wife answered the door and took Gustavo's hand and held it a moment too long and then turned in such a way as to brush her left breast against Gustavo's right elbow, Madeline looked at Bernard Allande and asked, "Thighs like fresh baked bread?"

Bernard grinned: "Who can resist fresh baked bread?"

Madeline again reaches for the sack of coal.

"You hear?" asks a voice in the dark, behind the villa where dead vines flourish, where toads burrow into the soil beneath the paper sacks of coal stacked at one end of the rotting pergola.

Madeline leans toward the voice but sees nothing – only darkness, and here and there within that darkness a deeper darkness where small shadows gather in the large shadow of night.

"Hear?" she asks.

The night does not answer, and for a moment Madeline thinks she is insane: not uniquely insane but commonly insane like so many others – like Stefano, like her mother – a dull insanity of spectral voices and tired delusions and the ugly face of loneliness limping alongside and sneering. The possibility dismays her.

> *Dear Gustavo: What is the point of being insane if it is a shared insanity? What is the point of losing one's mind if it is lost among so many others? My insanity, my madness, my fury must be unique because you – source of my insanity, my madness, my fury – are unique, rare, nonpareil. When you die there will be no others, if God is merciful.*

A twig snaps. The voice again rises out of the darkness: *"Il pianto della terra."*

Madeline peers deeper into the night, at a shadow gliding across the villa wall. *"Pianto?"*

The shadow halts and sighs, *"Sí, pianto."* And there follows a feigned weeping that only slightly resembles the groaning of the earth but is haunting nevertheless.

"Crying," says Madeline.

"Crying," repeats the shadow. *"Pianto."*

Madeline steps out from under the pergola into the dry weeds and moves toward the swaying shadow that turns at the sound of Madeline's approaching footsteps. Madeline can see now the white face of Angelina peering out from under a black cloak. Though her eyes stare fixedly at Madeline, there is a milkiness to them, an emptiness even more vast than the emptiness of Madeline's eyes.

"You hear?" the old woman interrupts.

Madeline moves closer to Angelina, close enough to smell her sad odor of burnt oil and sweat and urine, and says, "Yes, I hear it."

"You know why *il pianto?* Why the crying?"

"Because everything is dead."

Angelina chuckles hoarsely, shakes her head no. She scratches her nose and then picks it and wipes her finger on her cloak. She sighs wearily, "The dead is dead, the sleeping is sleeping. They have no *tormento.* But I, you, *la terra* – we feel more the cold because we have not the sleep and not the death and so we have *il pianto.*"

"Not I," says Madeline. "I do not cry."

The old woman grins wide, revealing rotting teeth and black gaps where teeth should be. She reaches out and finds Madeline's face that is red and stinging with cold, and searches it with her short dry fingers until they find Madeline's eyes which she presses shut. "Not here you cry, no." She drags her fingers down Madeline's face and neck, sniffing closely, loudly, like a dog, like Topi – down to Madeline's breasts upon which she flatly spreads her hands, saying, "Here," and pats twice, "here is *il pianto.*" She taps her nose once. "I smell. I do not see but I smell."

Madeline tries to withdraw, but Angelina binds her tight and whispers, "You think your heart is dead, Signora Rivera, but it is not dead. Listen. Smell. *La terra* is not dead, but cold and crying. Your heart is cold. My heart is cold. They cry. They wait for warm that not come never. Only death come, but *troppo lento, lento.*"

"Slow."

Angelina chuckles hoarsely. "Too much slow." Snot runs from her nose down to her lips.

"I do not wish to die," says Madeline with a vehemence that causes the old woman to lean back against the rough stone wall of the villa. "I wish to kill."

Angelina grins. "So you kill me."

"What?"

The old woman gropes for Madeline's hands and finds them and brings them to her neck of rolling flesh. "Kill me, *la madonna della morte*," and she presses Madeline's hands tight over her pulse.

Madeline tries to tug her hands free.

"Kill me," taunts the old woman, breaking into a fiendish cackle. "Kill me!"

Madeline braces her left foot against the villa and pulls and pulls and pulls until her hands break free and she stumbles backward and falls among the dry weeds, staring incredulously at Angelina who bursts with a gaping laughter, her face streaming with tears and thrown back toward the black sky. "*La madonna della morte!* Ha ha! You can not kill even one old woman who want the death!"

Madeline pants among the dry weeds, above the sleeping bugs and toads, upon the earth that groans.

Angelina raises her skirt above her waist, revealing thick naked legs marred by cuts and scabs and bruises.

Stefano's voice cries out, "Angelina!"

Angelina lets the skirt drop and feels her way along the wall of the villa – a laughing shadow slipping away into the winter night. Before she turns and finally disappears into darkness, she pauses to stare blindly at the northern hills where silence sweeps down like wind. "Some day you want death," nods Angelina. "You want but it no come, and then you cry." She taps her nose, nods again. "This, I smell."

Madeline says, "You smell the past."

The day Gustavo left – perhaps only minutes after he'd walked out, taking nothing but a bag of clothes, two first-class tickets to Rome, and $148,001 –

Madeline stood over a drawing ruined by spilled ink: ink spilled on a wet page, gray and bleeding, spilled by Gustavo's haste, and in his haste, his extreme haste, not even bothering to mop it up. She carefully folded the drawing, then carried it to the trash. Ink and water dripped onto the floor. She took a rag from the drawing table and bent down to wipe up the ink and water, and when she stood – after the ink and water were gone from the wooden floor and the floor was clean – when she stood up her heart leaped, then raced. It raced faster and faster. It raced so fast Madeline could not discern one beat from another. Her heart became no longer a pounding muscle but a place of heat inside her chest, the heat burning away her lungs so she could no longer breathe, and the heat boiling the blood in her head so she could no longer think, no longer think of anything except: *I am dying, I am dying of a broken heart*, and she stared at the rag stained with spilled ink and prayed to God it was true: *Dear God, let me die, let me die here and now with a rag in my hands and my hands stained with ink.*

But the moment she craved death, no longer feared it, her heart lurched, clenched like a fist, then began to slow until it was beating a perfect rhythm, even and strong.

DEAR MADDI, CIAO AND THANKS. GUSTAVO

"Shit," she wept, "shit, shit, shit," and crumpled the note and pressed her face into the ink-stained rag and dropped to her knees on the hard wooden floor and collapsed there, supine, arms flung wide, staring at the black spots on the rag that now lay over her face blinding her eyes from the vision of emptiness, the silence of Gustavo's absence humming in her ears – a humming like the humming of fluorescent lights, yes, Gustavo's absence epitomized by the ugly humming of fluorescent lights just before they flicker and die.

Madeline screamed, pleading for death's return.

Death turned a deaf ear.

Dear Gustavo: The sky is cold cold cold above me. The earth is cold cold cold beneath me. So cold that what is not yet dead will soon die. Here I lay. I am not yet dead.

Dear Gustavo: I do not choose death. But I must confess: Should death choose me, I will not reject it.

Beside the pergola Madeline rests among the dry weeds, upon the cold cold cold earth, arms spread, eyes closed, waiting to be chosen. Her body quakes uncontrollably. Her teeth chatter. Time passes. Death does not come.

Topi comes – wheezing, limping, drooling. She sniffs Madeline's throat, ears, hair.

Madeline opens one eye and peeks out at Topi who squats and shivers in the dry weeds. "Go away," she tells her, "I'm waiting for death."

Topi whimpers.

"Death is shy, Topi. He won't come with you standing guard over me."

Topi grins upon hearing her name and wobbles closer and lowers her head and licks Madeline's face.

Madeline cannot help herself: She smiles.

– three –

And so it is true: Death skulks everywhere in Bagno di Tristezza.

December 14. Tuesday or Wednesday or Saturday. Names of days no longer matter.

Massimo stands shivering behind the police captain who bends over Angelina frozen where she fell: beneath the spigot across the road, and the sweet spring water frozen, too, in a glistening cascade from the spigot's mouth down to Angelina's corpse glazed in a rippling sheet of ice upon which the captain knocks as if upon an ordinary door.

Of course, no one answers.

Yet Angelina's blind eyes – frozen open in irritated astonishment beneath a quarter-inch of ice – are shifted slightly to the right, toward the dead olive tree where Stefano leans against the gray trunk, drinking Chianti, squinting resentfully at Angelina's corpse, as if expecting it – no, daring it to thaw and rise up shouting accusations.

But Angelina will never rise up. And anyway, one of the neighbors has taken it upon herself to speak for the dead: whispering to the captain information she considers factual, unconcerned that she is exaggerating, reshaping the truth into a jury already salivating with the hunger to indict. The woman whispers and points here and there to where the flesh is exposed upon Angelina's corpse beneath the ice: a bruise, a scratch, a scab. She whispers, glances at Stefano who swills and squints his resentment. The captain frowns and nods.

Massimo stands off to the side, shivering, writing barely legible words in a small leather notebook, softly humming di Lasso's *Timor et Tremor* – until Madeline appears at the heavy wooden gate of the garden, smiling faintly, shivering faintly, bare legs white below the hem of her black coat. At which point Massimo's heart lurches inside his chest, blood already pulsing toward his cock, cold fleeing. The music in his throat does not stop as he closes his notebook and steps around Angelina's frozen corpse and walks past the neighbor-woman and the captain conspiring, past Stefano squinting, and across the road to the wooden gate that Madeline swings wide. She turns and walks through the garden, halts at the villa door, looking over her shoulder to be certain Massimo follows.

Massimo follows. Without glancing back at the dead or the dead to be.

Dear Gustavo: The shape of waiting is the taste of spit, the scent of heat, the breadth of cock slick with blood.

Behind a clothes rack hung with fur coats and taffeta gowns and satin slips, behind the armoires and hat boxes and shoe boxes and cedar chests, behind the hollow shells of dead moths and wasps and beetles, Massimo slides his hands up Madeline's thighs and clutches the cool soft cheeks of her bottom, and lifts her up, and gently – or perhaps not so gently – shoves her backward against the wall upon which hangs a tapestry depicting a bloody Medieval hunting scene: horses and hounds chasing, wounding, tearing into deer whose ripped throats gush red and silent. And Madeline breathes, "*Sí, sí, sí,* Massimo," while he dips a finger into her menstrual blood and paints it upon her clitoris while she wraps her legs around his waist, her arms around his neck, and eases herself onto his cock while he buries his face in the pulse at her throat and hums, and thrusts, and hums.

Accidental music.

Madeline does not complain.

Was Gustavo a good lover?

Ask the clerk at the shoe store. Ask the conductor's wife. Ask the gallery owner. Ask the dry cleaner's daughter. Ask the soprano from the opera chorus.

"Was Gustavo a good lover?" Madeline asked the soprano from the opera chorus.

The soprano strained against the backstage cacophony of scales – up and down and up and down, voices singing and instruments playing – strained and tilted her lovely head toward Madeline and said, "I beg your pardon?"

Madeline stared at the soprano's neck, at the white skin over her throat over her bones over her vocal chords that could be so easily severed, rendered useless and silent, with a single gnash of the teeth.

"I beg your pardon?" the soprano repeated.

Madeline did not ask again. She did not ask again because she did not want to know what she already knew: Yes.

Dear Gustavo: Yes, you were a good lover, and they all would have agreed – not because you made them come again and again, sacrificing your own carnal pleasure for the sake of theirs for you never sacrificed anything, certainly not your own pleasure, but because your beautiful mouth on their mouth, your beautiful tongue down their throats, your beautiful hands on their breasts, your beautiful cock in their cunts...your beauty, Gustavo, and that alone, transformed them. In the brief moment that their bodies possessed your beauty, they all shuddered and turned to gold.

Dear Gustavo: Alchemy. Though your lovers would have stupidly cried: Love!

Madeline shudders and whispers into Massimo's black hair, "Alchemize me. Make me gold."

Madeline awoke to find herself alone in the night of another country, in the yellow bed in the yellow bedroom. It was not the first time she had awakened alone, the clock on the night table having spun far past midnight, and the silence in the night cold and terrible as if she had awakened into death instead of ordinary night. Ordinary, except for her aloneness – not the first time, however, no.

But the first time, yes, when Madeline did not lay awake thinking. In fact, she did not think at all. She got out of bed and dressed and drove downtown to the opera house that loomed darkly in the darkness. The streets surrounding it were empty except for a narrow alley by the rear door outside of which a small white car was parked. She pulled up behind the small white car, got out, felt the metal hood. It was cold. She walked to the rear door and found it propped open with a simple matchbook jimmied between the lock and jamb. Inside the opera house was dark, so dark Madeline dared not step further for fear of stumbling upon something unpleasant.

Madeline did not need to step further to stumble upon something unpleasant: The music of sex is distinctive, though it sometimes resembles the music of murder – again, that narrow gap between pleasure and pain, between truly living and truly dying.

Madeline, who did not know music the way Gustavo knew music, knew the music of Gustavo fucking, and so was drawn to it like a rat to a piper's flute, not thinking, thinking not at all, simply moving forward in the darkness toward the music of Gustavo fucking a woman turning to gold. She did not think, not even when she stumbled, literally, upon something solid and lost her balance and toppled headlong into the darkness, grabbing at air as she fell and then grabbing at something cold and slick and metal that came tumbling down upon her as she hit the floor, something that sliced across her right shoulder, through her sweater, through her flesh. Did not think even then, think to scream or cry or shout, still straining toward the music of Gustavo fucking although the music had of course stopped.

And then she thought: *For godsake, Madeline, do not let them find you here bleeding on the floor like some stupid clumsy goddamn spy.*

And so she did not move, barely breathed, while Gustavo and the nearly-gold lover briefly searched for the source of the noise, and then tired of the search, and then went back to fucking until Gustavo's nearly-gold lover was fully gold. And Madeline did not leave and did not move and did not weep. But she bled. She bled upon the floor and she thought: *But it could be anyone, couldn't it? Anyone could sound like Gustavo fucking a woman to gold. Bernard Allande, for example. It could be Bernard. Yes, Bernard. Not Gustavo. No, Gustavo is mine.*

Massimo runs his lips across the scar on Madeline's right shoulder.

After the emergency room doctor put twelve stitches in Madeline's shoulder, after Madeline sat in her car staring up at the black windows of the apartment for over an hour, after she finally went inside and opened the door to the yellow bedroom and found Gustavo asleep alone in their bed, after she lay down beside him and he awoke and kissed her once before going back to sleep, after she took four pain killers instead of two and went to sleep and did not wake up until the following evening when she again woke alone in the yellow bedroom, alone except for a single blood-red rose in a vase on the nightstand and a note that read, *"Te amo,* Maddi" – after all this and certainly more, Madeline thought to herself: *It was Bernard, of course. Not Gustavo.*

Krissy said, "Of course it was Gustavo!"
Madeline said, "It was Bernard Allande."
Krissy said, "It was Gustavo, and you know it! Why won't you admit it was Gustavo?"
Madeline said, "Why won't you shut up!"
Krissy slowly stood and put on her coat and threw her purse over her shoulder. She dropped a twenty on the restaurant table and said, "You're so fucking blind, Madeline. You deserve what you get."

Massimo is standing in the midst of them all before he realizes he is standing in the midst of them all. Every policeman from Bagno di Tristezza's day shift has come to witness the frozen glory of Angelina, less blind in death perhaps than in life, black angry clouds

sweeping down from the north hills, clouds undoubt-
edly full of snow and terrible wind and a deep vengeful
cold, at which Massimo stares, smiling and humming,
humming.

"...*sangue sulle vostre mani!*"

Massimo hears the words as if from an irrelevant
distance, unlike Stefano who quickly glances down to
see if there is indeed blood on his hands. There is not.
Only the red of inflammation where his handcuffs rub
too tightly against his wrist bones.

"*C'é sangue sulle vostre mani,*" Paulo repeats, this
time touching Massimo on the shoulder to wake him
from his reverie.

Massimo looks down at his hands, his bloody
hands, and is for a moment bewildered. He wonders if
he has cut himself somewhere between the room full of
fancy clothes and here – on the old wooden gate,
perhaps? – and he instinctively raises a hand to his face
and sniffs his fingers and knows, then, it is Madeline's
blood on his hands – blood, and sex – and he smiles.

"*C'é niente,*" he says, waving Paulo away, then
calmly walks to the spigot and breaks the icicle holding
back the flood of good spring water and washes the
blood from his hands while everyone – Paulo who
stops breathing, and the police captain who stops ges-
ticulating, and the five police officers who stop ducking
the gesticulations, and the coroner who stops pulling
on his rubber gloves, and the coroner's photographer
who stops shooting close-ups of Angelina's frozen eye-
balls for his private collection, and the neighbor-
woman who stops praying, and Stefano who stops
cursing – everyone stops and watches dumbfounded as
the water lightly tinted with Madeline's blood washes
from Massimo's fingers and over Angelina's corpse

whose shroud of ice cracks slowly, audibly, head to toe.

And in the brief moment before everyone begins shouting all at once, Topi hobbles from the wood shed, between the legs of the living, to the spigot where she drinks from the pool of good spring water in which Angelina thaws and Massimo stands, black polished shoes half-submerged, now calmly drying his hands on the trousers of his police uniform.

Above it all, Madeline huddles naked inside a black coat, watching from her silent aerie of stone, windows thrown wide toward the approaching storm.

VII. Nocturne:
L'heure verte

Assuming there is a boundary between dreams and waking, how wide is that boundary? A gulf? A cleft? A thread so thin it collapses with the slightest breath?

The slightest breath of a Parisian girl no more than a child, the girl, Parisian, collapses Gustavo's dream of burning watercolors dissolving to darkness like paper dissolving to flame: "Awaken! Awaken, please, Monsieur, it is time to go home! The storm is coming, it is coming soon!"

The little Parisian hand, soft and dirty, black beneath the nails, strokes his cheek bristling with new whiskers painful to the touch, the whiskers, and so the little Parisian hand recoils, pauses a moment before returning to his face with such force that the imprint of her palm and five fingers will remain there on the skin of his cheek until dawn, which is yet three hours away.

"Awaken, Monsieur!"

Slap.

"Awaken to avoid the coming storm!"

His head rolls so loosely upon his neck that when the Parisian girl-child slaps him again, it flops backward against the pocked marble of the statue upon which he sits – the collision of skull and stone audible, a dull thump, as if someone were testing a cantaloupe for ripeness.

But Gustavo's head is not a cantaloupe. It is skin and blood and bone and brain. Sleeping brain, sodden mind. Sodden and dulled by black market absinthe and – *Ah yes! but my god why also?* – hashish.

He opens one eye and sees nothing. Squints, strains hard, sees a polished black shoe – his own? for he cannot feel his feet or legs. Sees the moon reflected upon the shoe's shiny wet surface.

Again the little Parisian hand rebounds – "Awaken! Awaken!" – and there is now so much force behind each blow, so much violent energy for a child, for a woman even, that it becomes clear the Parisian girl-child takes pleasure in striking him, though the stiffness of his whiskers causes her pain, her palm flushed red and hot and stinging with pain, yet she cocks the whole of her little arm to strike once more, her hand coiled this time into a fist.

If I am dreaming I wish to wake. If I am awake I wish to dream.

A figure hovers at the periphery of consciousness. Hovers, hovers, insisting on its own presence.

It is Madeline, of course. There, just to his left. Madeline hovering, insisting, laughing at the hollow thump of his skull upon the statue. And the statue, too, is Madeline–though here she is winged and silent, a vengeful angel with a determined gaze, the gaze that tells him it is her, Madeline, always determined to get what she wants and always getting what she wants through her determination.

What does Madeline want?

The moon on my shoe.

Slap.

149

My cock in her cunt.

Slap.

The blood on my tongue.

Slap.

He spits. Blood runs down his chin and drops into his lap at which he now stares in horror: Blood on his cock that hangs limp outside his unzipped trousers. And his trousers wet with semen. His own, he presumes, he hopes. And the moon is so bright on his shoe, on his lap, on his blood, on his eyelids that burn with moonlight. He rolls his head to the left and backward, and looks up at the moon which is not the moon but a streetlight, of course, for the sky is black with clouds and smells of wind and rain, and sounds of thunder, not Madeline's laughter, no, not laughter at all but thunder there to his left, advancing, encroaching upon this dream, this nightmare from which he cannot cannot cannot seem to wake.

And to his right the Parisian girl-child holds up his wallet with her little thumb and index finger, flaps the wallet through the air as if it were a bird, flying it past Gustavo's nose and squawking and grinning and squawking.

He reaches for it.

The wallet flies just beyond his fingertips.

Reaches again.

Flies away.

Reaches, flies.

This absurd game continues for an absurd length of time. Until his nausea swells from his belly to his throat and he can no longer follow the bird, his wallet, with his eyes for his eyes are bleeding it seems and the pain of their bleeding explodes as he doubles over – over his shiny moonlit shoe – and retches and retches and retches until there is nothing more to retch, and retches nothing longer still.

The girl-child, bored, perhaps disgusted, removes all the francs from his wallet and tosses the wallet into the puddle of vomit and counts the francs and tucks them inside her little Parisian dress and looks up at the sky and says, before disappearing into whatever dream, whatever green nightmare she stepped out of, says, "*Adieu, Monsieur, adieu.* The storm at last is here."

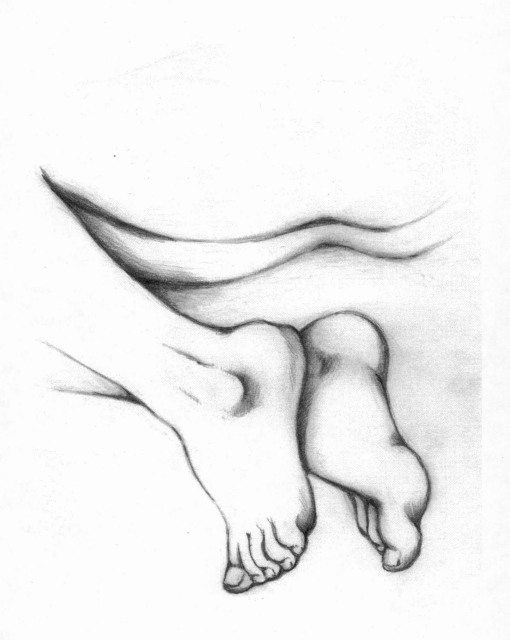

VIII. Allegro mosso
Pietà

– one –

The rain in the hollow of Jesus' lap freezes, expands, splits the old wood along the length of its grain. Thus a fissure sprouts from Jesus' groin to Mary's breast where a red bleeding heart sits exposed upon the blue of her gown.

The 15th of December: a hellish cold, an evil wind.

The pietà topples.

Mary's wooden eyes stare at the winter sky as if stunned by the dead weight of Jesus upon her lap, as if she too will die, here beneath the gray-black Italian sky, die in Stefano's imaginary garden, crushed by the heaviness of Jesus upon her lap.

Pity, pity, ah pity!

Death, after all, is such a burden to the living.

Dear Gustavo: Let yours be a burden to me.

The tower is so cold, so continuously cold, that the coals in the stove serve no purpose but to burn what is no longer needed: sketches and drawings and paintings of Gustavo. Madeline can no longer precisely remember his beautiful face, beautiful body, and her artwork does not do him justice – *That's my job* – and so she

153

feeds his images to the hot red coals and for a moment
is warmed by the heat of the short-lived flames.

The young clerk at *la posta* takes Madeline's letter,
weighs it, says, *Something-something-something lire* and
then fixes her eyes directly upon Madeline's, though
this is a difficult thing to do: fixing upon gray eyes
empty and cold like a faithless death, a warning of
what will surely come to the unrepentant.

Madeline hands a tattered slip of paper to the clerk:
Io sono sorda. Per favore, me lo scriva.

The clerk takes the note and purses her lips as she
methodically tears the note into little pieces and
scatters the pieces over the counter like confetti.
Madeline's expression remains unchanged which
surprises, then disturbs the young woman, and so she
is less confident when she recites, "You are not...deaf,"
faltering on the word "deaf" which she pronounces in
two syllables – *day-eef* – and then blushes, knowing she
has erred, and so surreptitiously glances inside the
stamp drawer where she has taped the phrase
rehearsed a hundred times, "You are not deaf, you are
American," thus concluding her indictment with
bathos, the final sputter of a deflated balloon.

Madeline laughs – a reflex, like laughing at
someone tripping over their own shoelace. "Yes," says
Madeline, "American. *La madonna nera. La madonna della
morte.*"

The clerk shifts her eyes downward and to the left.
She tries again to look Madeline in the eye but cannot.
Instead she looks at the topmost button of Madeline's
black coat, a black button so shiny the clerk can see
her face reflected in it, reduced to the size of
Madeline's thumbnail.

Madeline pats the clerk's left hand which the clerk immediately withdraws and tucks safely away under the counter.

"So then," Madeline says, business-like, and pulls out a handful of bills. She drops them onto the counter and empties her pockets of coins as well. "Enough?" she asks. *"Basta?"*

The clerk looks at the lire, then suspiciously at Madeline, then slowly begins counting the lire which is of course too much, as Madeline knows, as does the clerk who separates the bills and coins into two stacks: the exact amount of postage stacked upon Madeline's letter, and the remaining lire – eight, nine, ten times the amount of *la posta*ge – stacked upon the counter. The clerk slides this second stack toward Madeline.

Madeline slides it back. "Keep it."

The clerk again slides the lire across the counter. *"Troppo."*

Madeline again slides it back. "Yes, too much, I know. But this is my last letter, *capisce?* There will be no more letters, no more postcards. I have a feeling it is all coming to an end. So keep the money. Buy yourself something nice. Something beautiful."

The clerk sits uncomprehending, glancing back and forth between Madeline and the money. After a long moment Madeline snatches the young woman by the wrist and pins it to the wooden counter and grabs the excess lire and stuffs it into the clerk's now trembling hand and folds the clerk's now trembling fingers over the lire, and says loudly, slowly, with neither kindness nor malice, *"Per tu, capisce?* For you."

The young woman sits staring at the lire in her still trembling hand. When she looks up Madeline is gone.

Dear Gustavo: I have a feeling it's all coming to an end.

The clerk pastes stamps on Madeline's letter, drops Madeline's payment into the drawer, tucks Madeline's excess lire into the sleeve of her shirt. Grins.

> Bagno di Tristezza, Italy
> December 15

Dear Cliff:

I have a feeling it is all coming to an end. A strong feeling like an odor carried inside this grieving wind that bites so fiercely at my face and hands. The odor is bitter. Thus, the end will be bitter. We cannot, should not expect more.

This morning the church bell pealed at an odd dark hour. Too early. Before matins. Before the sun rose without color over this frozen valley of dying. The bell pealed, an insidious knell: 'Ma-de-line! Ma-de-line! Ma-de-line!' until I got out of bed and went to the window and opened it and screamed, 'For godsake, what?' And then the bell went silent, its answer to me.

I wanted to pray then, or sing, to end this awful silence more hollow because it follows such an abundance of music. I wanted to drop to my knees and ask God to have pity on me, have pity on me and let the waiting and the silence come to an end. But I couldn't. The floor was too hard, too cold, and the word 'pity' caught in my throat.

(Does the desire to pray constitute praying? Does the desire for an end to suffering lead to an end to suffering?)

I think you will never receive this letter because you are already on your way here. I think you have found Gustavo.

Madeline

Outside, not even a bird song.

Dear Gustavo: Like you, winter has swallowed the music of living.

Here, the pitiable suburb, Bagno di Tristezza: steeped in decline, and the decline soundless, not even the howling of skinny dogs or the knocking of rats in garbage cans or the sighs of people dreaming of another country, another life. Houses shuttered against the cold. No movement except smoke rising from chimneys, and smoke rises without a sound.

Here, the olive grove: a graveyard haunted by ghosts of the mute and misshapen. Unpicked olives fallen and rotted or frozen in the grass. The grass dry and bent over the earth by the ceaseless wind that has finally ceased, having relinquished its role to the great cold silence of winter's heart.

Here, the old church: stucco quietly crumbling, the bell tower as inert as the spire with its iron cross. The heavy wooden door of the church groans as the old gray priest steps out, shoulders round, head bent, feet shuffling upon the cobblestones.

"Giorno!" Madeline calls.

157

The old priest freezes like a frightened opossum, moving neither forward nor backward, moving not at all except to slowly raise a hand to his mouth, which is agape, and to weave there a tiny cross. Madeline steps toward him. He quickly turns and shuffles back up the walkway to the church door, which he strains to open, groaning as it groans.

"Scuzi!" Madeline calls.

The old priest gives a final grunt and the door swings free.

"Can you hear me?" Madeline asked in another life. The confessional was cold and hard and her tailbone already ached from having waited so long.

"I hear you," replied the priest. "What have you come to confess?"

"Love," Madeline replied.

"Love?"

"Yes. I am in love with my husband."

A long pause. The priest cleared his throat. "Please explain your meaning."

"I love him too much."

"Your husband."

"Yes."

"But is it possible to love too much?"

"Yes, is it?"

"Well," the priest hesitated; the confessional creaked from his squirming, "if we love someone or something more than God –"

"I do. I love my husband more than God, more than myself, more than life. I would die for my husband. I would kill for my husband. I would go to hell for my husband."

"Indeed," the priest said unkindly, "you're well on your way."

"So it *is* a sin to love my husband this much."

"More than God? Yes."

"Then forgive me for I cannot stop myself."

"But you must."

"I can't."

"You must at least try."

Madeline closed her eyes and thought of Gustavo who was beautiful, then she thought of God who was unseen. She weighed each vision in her heart, and her heart like a ship listed toward Gustavo, toward manifest beauty, and she repeated, "Have pity on me, Father, and on my husband too, for his beauty is greater than God's."

"Then you don't understand beauty," said the priest.

Madeline opens the wrought iron gate to the churchyard and moves up the cobbled walkway. As she reaches for the door she hears a loud click and grinding of metal: a big key in a big lock. The door doesn't open.

Madeline knocks, "Hello? Hello?" and knocks again. She sits upon the cold stone steps and presses her lips to the keyhole. She whispers, "Forgive me, Father, for what I am about to do."

She leaves the churchyard and walks across the road and stands upon Via Veleno that here overlooks the valley, and beyond the valley in the distance: Florence, upon which the sun shines unobscured as if it were another continent, another season.

"After Rome," said Madeline, naked in the yellow bedroom in another country another continent another season, "we'll drive to Florence and find a room over-looking the Arno."

Gustavo, naked and dour, replied, "Bernard Allande says to me the Arno stinks like shit."

"It's Bernard who stinks like shit," snapped Madeline. She jumped out of bed and went to the window and stared out at the falling leaves. "Winter's coming soon," she said, calmer. "We'll go to Italy where it's warm, where the sun shines always. We'll leave all of this and Bernard Allande behind and we'll miss the winter entirely and be happy again."

After a long silence, she sat down on the bed and peered into Gustavo's unhappy face that was either asleep or pretending to be asleep – she no longer cared which – and slid a finger from Gustavo's forehead to his foot and whispered, "Beautiful man."

"Then you don't understand beauty," said the priest.

She looks at the blue sky above Florence then lifts her head and looks at the gray sky above Bagno di Tristezza. Gray not blue, as if the world through which she marked time were smoldering.

Dear Gustavo: Have pity on me for my heart no longer lists toward you for it has sunk to the bottom of the sea in which the world has drowned in the silence of your absence and the absence of a silent God of perpetual silence and winter and death.

Not even a birdsong.

– two –

As it was then: sometimes: orchid on the sill, candles on the table, scent of musk and amber, music flowing down the walls like honey.

"Come here," Gustavo would say. And Madeline would go to him and he would spread his knees and she would step inside the space he had made for her there between his thighs. *"Que linda,"* he would whisper, running his hands from her ankles to her hips, "so pretty." And he would kiss her belly, the small basin of flesh between her pubis and left thigh, and she would shiver with pleasure.

Sometimes this, then. Sometimes not.

Sometime on the evening of Bernard Allande's farewell concerto, only days before Gustavo fled, Gustavo sat on the edge of the yellow bed, beautiful in his black suit, black hair slicked back, legs crossed, smoking a cigarillo, watching Madeline brush her hair in front of the long mirror, skin of her back white, translucent it seemed against the black velvet of her dress.

Gustavo looked at his watch, then tamped out his cigarillo. "Come here," he said.

Madeline stopped brushing and looked at Gustavo's reflection in the mirror, surprised to hear what she had not heard for so long. She tried to appear nonchalant, smiled coyly, "We'll be late."

"No. Come here."

Madeline set down her brush and went to Gustavo who uncrossed his legs and spread his knees wide. She stepped between them. He slid his hands from her ankles up to her thighs above her stockings where her exposed flesh was soft and warm, slightly damp. *"Que linda,"* he said, and Madeline waited for him to lift her dress, kiss her belly, kiss the basin near her thigh.

But he did not.

Instead, he clutched her hips in his big hands and tenderly laid his head against the velvet over her belly as if listening there, and whispered, "Wife. Wife." And still Madeline waited – for what now she did not know – with her hands on Gustavo's head, an incidental benediction.

Then Gustavo surreptitiously checked his watch, lifted his head, patted Madeline twice and said, "Time for Bernard's swan song."

"Swan song," Madeline says to no one but the pigeon dead upon the cold mud of Via Veleno. Thus:

Here, the pigeon: still warm to the touch, pink eyes shining, wings spread as if it might again rise up and take flight. But it will not fly. It will freeze solid in this cold Italian air, a feathered stone tossed to the side of the road, then will thaw in the distant warmth of spring, then will succumb to insects and mammals and rot.

"Swan song," Madeline repeats. Song of death, song of decay. *Song without words:* Mendelssohn.

There were rumors: Bernard Allande's fingers had grown fat and slow. Only a matter of time, they said, before the cello became his nemesis rather than his ally. And then, they said, poor Bernard Allande, they said, then what would he do?

"Die," announced Bernard Allande.

Gustavo laughed. "You will not die. It is arthritis, not cancer."

"Ah, but I wish it was cancer," said Bernard Allande, studying his hands pressed flat on the dressing table, fingers splayed. "Who will want to fuck me after the music is gone?"

As Bernard had requested, there was no one else in his dressing room except Gustavo and Madeline. But the room was filled with colossal bouquets so that there was little space to move, and breathing was encumbered by the close scent of hundreds of roses.

"Perhaps you could compose after your retirement," Madeline offered, dully, since by now she did not care at all for Bernard, disliked him, in fact, suspected him of duplicity and turpitude, but she affected geniality for the sake of Gustavo who by now cared for Bernard quite a lot.

Bernard Allande winced at the word *retirement* and looked up from his swollen fingers to sneer at Madeline's reflection in the mirror. "I am afraid, *cherie*, that composing is not my forte." And he spun around in his chair and snapped at Gustavo, "You, at least, have that! That and your pretty, pretty face." Then he looked at Madeline and smiled, eyes narrowed, "Did you know, Madeline Rivera, that your husband is very much the *Griffonneur du musique*, that he has dreams – quite large dreams, *bien plus* – to one day make his debut as a composer?" He paused long enough to catch a faint shadow of surprise upon Madeline's face, though she tried to hide it, and so he added, "But of course you knew this, Madeline Rivera. You are his wife!" And he laughed.

Madeline looked at Gustavo who looked at his watch and then at Bernard and said, not without rancor, "Time for your swan song, Monsieur Allande."

Here, the pale reeds: so dry they are closer to dust than water. But in spring there will be water flowing through them and they will sway and perhaps even bend, liquid as they will have grown.

To become liquid, fluid as time and thus immutable, that is the aim.

They, the rumormongers, had to give Bernard Allande credit: If there was sickness in his joints, it was difficult to discern by his performance. His program was grueling for even a healthy musician. Yet, he played with such passion and finesse that even Madeline wept during his encore of Saint-Saëns' *The Swan.*

And Bernard wept, too, though it was not so much emotion that brought tears to his eyes but pain. After over an hour of Bach and Dvorak and Mendelsohnn, accompanied only by piano or no accompaniment at all, Bernard's anti-inflammatory medication was no longer effective; his joints began to swell. And although he had swallowed enough pain killers to numb but not inhibit, they too had worn off by the time the audience leapt to their feet, hand-stinging applause, screaming *"Encore! Encore!"* which Bernard Allande, of course, could not refuse. And so: *The Swan* performed with passion and finesse – not a note misplaced, not a phrase misspoken – tears streaming from eyes pinched shut against unrelenting pain, and no one truly aware of his valor except perhaps Gustavo who gazed at Bernard weeping upon the stage, gazed with an expression Madeline could not precisely define for Gustavo had never before gazed at her with such an expression, and for the briefest moment – a moment so brief it was forgotten as soon as it passed – she knew he never would.

December 16. Heels on mud. Hands burning with cold.

Madeline glances over her shoulder at sunny Florence off in the distance…

We'll go to Italy where it's warm, where the sun shines always. We'll leave all of this and Bernard Allande behind and we'll miss the winter entirely and be happy again.

…and spits. And considers:

Afterward, during the farewell party at the restaurant, Bernard kissed Gustavo full on the lips, lingering there until Gustavo shoved him away and spit and wiped his mouth with the back of his hand.

Madeline halts on Via Veleno and stares down at a toad squashed flat and perfectly preserved in the frozen mud. Halts and considers:

Rising to the surface is an answer to a question she cannot formulate. She can feel it surfacing in her mind like a corpse, drowned body tangled among algae and suddenly freed, freed and bloated and thus rising slowly to the surface of Madeline's mind.

Bernard Allande – drunk, very drunk – leaned sideways as if about to topple into Madeline's lap but instead opened his mouth, and his tongue rolled out, and he licked Madeline from neck to ear.

Madeline said, "Pig!"

To which Bernard responded: *"Oui, ma petite moule, je suis un cochon.* But don't you know how smart are pigs?" And he let loose a mirthful laugh, head thrown back, teeth gleaming with saliva, hands pressed over his chest as if to keep his heart from bursting forth.

Madeline tried to flee but Bernard grabbed her arm and gripped it tight and held her in her chair. He put his mouth close to her ear and whispered, "You are lovely, Madeline Rivera, lovely, yes. But I lick you with the hope of tasting Gustavo on your skin," and he sat back to watch Madeline's response.

Madeline's response was to wrench her arm free and leap out of her chair and glower into Bernard Allande's face which bore no expression whatsoever – neither mirth nor sobriety nor sincerity nor even hatred: a frightening blankness. She continued staring as her own face filled with blood, the bloody red of fury. And when her face was full, so full that even her eyes seemed to bleed with rage, she slapped Bernard so hard he fell out of his chair, catching himself with his left hand before hitting the floor – a stupid reflex for a musician, protecting his ass over his hand – catching himself there in a homely position, like an insect, a spider about to be squashed.

Toad squashed flat and frozen in the mud, framed between Madeline's black patent shoes.

Everyone in the restaurant – musicians, all – went silent and turned to watch Bernard Allande pick himself up from the floor, and brush the cuffs of his

tuxedo though they were quite clean. Turned to watch
Gustavo go after Madeline who was walking toward
the door, palm of her hand still stinging, head held high
and turned slightly to the side in order to hear
Gustavo, as he passed Bernard, ask, "Why? Why
now?"

Considers and glances up from the flattened toad to
see more clearly, more precisely into the past, but
instead sees Topi at the bottom of the hill, sleeping
with a stillness far more chilling than the winter air.
Thus, the surfacing corpse of an answer to an
unknown question sinks again and is lost among the
dark infested waters of Madeline's memory.

She hurries down the steep slope at the bottom of
which Topi is curled in the dry grass alongside the
road.

"Topi?" she whispers, gently touching the balding
head which is cold, the curved spine which is cold, the
cold hair coming loose and falling among the dry grass
now that there is no wind to carry it away.

"Ah, Topi!" Madeline sighs.

And something inside her – something long frozen
and as dead as this old dog beside this frozen mud road
– breaks like ice on a spigot.

— three —

He, too, longs for another life, another country where winter is a memory, death a routine sleep, and gray absent except in the irises of his lover's eyes.

His grandfathers were policemen. His father was a policeman. Therefore, he is a policeman, but he does not know what this means. Purchased uniform. Borrowed skin. Skin that grows tighter each year as he grows away from what it is he does not understand. Tighter, until it chokes him. *Or splits*, thinks Massimo, tapping the jar inside of which a homely caterpillar shifts toward the beauty for which it was destined.

Here on the gray cement terrace of his small gray apartment in gray Bagno di Tristezza birds alight on the leafless gray twigs of potted trees and flock to his feeders, but they are not exquisite birds. They are plain and gray. They twitter rather than sing. And beyond them, the backside of Bagno di Tristezza even more gray, more pitiable than the front: junked autos and furniture, overflowing garbage cans, cardboard boxes, pipes and poles and electrical wires sagging between one building and another. Gray, gray, gray. And a gray stench like death with its ashen face.

He picks up the jar and peers inside at the chrysalis suspended from a twig. *Release me*, he beseeches the woman with gray eyes, *rend this borrowed skin with the knife of your love.*

"I want tell you —"
"No, no!" Paulo cries wearily. "I want *to* tell you."

Massimo blushes, nods, fights the frustration building inside his borrowed skin. He furrows his brow with
renewed dedication and says, "I want *to* tell you…"

"That…" Paulo prompts.

"That you are pretty."

"Thank you!" Paulo chirps, batting his eyelashes
and dipping a limp wrist at Massimo.

Massimo laughs. Then sobers. "But what is this I'm
saying to her?" he asks in Italian.

"That she is pretty," replies Paulo.

"But it's not correct. It's not enough."

"Then what is enough?"

Massimo closes his eyes, imagines Madeline: her
scent, everywhere her softness. He opens his eyes and
stares at a place so distant it could be another country,
another life.

*Woman of the gray eyes, release me. Let this foreign skin
that binds me close to death split open, fall away from the heat
of your touch, the knife of your love.*

Paulo, mute and red-faced – embarrassed –
scratches his Dante nose and stares at the map of
Bagno di Tristezza, follows the red line of highway
through its heart until he disappears into the whiteness
of wall.

"Can you teach me to say these things?" Massimo
asks with an urgency that nearly breaks Paulo's heart.

"Sure," sighs Paulo, again scratching his big nose.

Flood of pain, flood of rage. Cold hide of a dead dog
wet with a flood of tears.

The police car passes the church as the old priest pokes his head out and cautiously surveys the churchyard before stepping onto the cobblestones and waving at the police car passing by.

Massimo waves back. Hums. Hums and practices: *Woman of the gray eyes, I need you.*

From the top of the slope that descends steeply toward Villa Ferramo, he sees at the bottom where the road curves sharply upward: Madeline curled in the dry grass. His heart stops. His breath stops. His car stops. And then he is out and running on the cold mud where he can now hear, with a mixture of relief and dread, Madeline's weeping: haunting, a combination of music and grief.

He gently takes her by the shoulders and lifts her from the dead dog and picks the stiff white hairs from her face, strokes her cheeks until her weeping subsides and she leans into him, shivering with cold and fatigue.

Woman of the gray eyes, he thinks but has not the courage to say, and so he hums softly the intermezzo from Mascagni's *Cavalleria Rusticana* as if it were merely a lullaby and he merely a man stripped of an ill-fitting uniform, rocking his gray-eyed lover to sleep in his arms.

Topi is buried in Stefano's imaginary garden, among the weeds that were never vegetables.

In the cold cold tower Madeline sits astride Massimo. Trembles. Takes his thick brown arms and crosses them over her breasts. Trembles. Closes her eyes.

"I want tell you…," whispers Massimo.

Madeline's eyes open.

"That I…to need that…you…," his voice fading to less than the gray light through the high tower windows.

"Please," says Madeline, dropping his arms, "don't try to speak English."

"Scuzi?"

She claps a hand over his mouth. "No English – *non inglese, per favore.*"

He removes her hand. *"Perché?"*

She rolls off him and snatches a cigarette from the pack on the floor and lights it and paces back and forth on the cold red tiles, bare feet slapping and stinging. Back and forth, back and forth, naked in front of the big mirror in which Massimo can see both sides of her, left and right equally lovely, coming and going.

"Because," she says, pacing and smoking, "when you speak comprehensible words I am reminded that you are a human being which reminds me that I am a human being – or was, once upon a time in another country, another life – and I do not wish to be reminded, do not wish to be human, Massimo, do not wish to feel anything more than what my body feels – desire and pleasure from fulfilled desire, and blood rushing to my sex and then back to my head, these things only, do you understand? These things and nothing more – except perhaps rage. Yes. No. I cannot afford to feel anything more. Not now, not when it is so close to the end, I am sure, close. I cannot cannot cannot." She stops to look at him. "Do you understand, Massimo? *Capisce?"*

Massimo shakes his head no.

Madeline grins and bends down and kisses him long and deep. "Beautiful ignorant man," she whispers, climbing back onto his lap.

Thus: Madeline and Massimo sitting face to face on the bed moving slowly against each other, one inside the other inside the other: cock in cunt, thumb in mouth, and the heat from their bodies nearly visible in the cold cold tower. Even after Madeline notices Stefano standing in the room, she does not stop moving against Massimo, does not take her thumb from his mouth, close as she is to coming. And Massimo, too, so close that his teeth bite down on her thumb gently but hard enough that Madeline moans. Stefano laughs.

Massimo jerks away from Madeline and pulls a blanket over his lap.

Stefano continues laughing as he tosses the telegram at the bed and walks out of the tower, laughing.

Silence descends. Clouds of breath in the air.

Massimo stares pensively at his belly. Runs a finger along a scratch that bleeds there on his belly. Imagines a chrysalis splitting open, falling away.

Madeline falls backward onto the bed. Sees the telegram that has settled like a bright yellow bird announcing the coming of spring.

DEAR MADELINE. GUSTAVO IS LIVING IN PARIS, NOT ALONE. IF TRAINS DON'T STRIKE I ARRIVE IN FLORENCE AT 14:25 HRS, 17 DEC. MAKE FINAL PLANS THEN. LONG TO SEE YOU TOUCH YOU SMELL YOU. DESTROY THIS. LOVE CLIFF.

Yes. It is all coming to an end.

Madeline swings the duffel bag over her shoulder and opens the door and steps out into the cold day.

"Wait!" Stefano cries. "Do not go, Signorina!"

Madeline lifts the rotting latch of the garden gate.

Stefano sticks his head out the door. "You stay here for free! Yes! For all ways!"

Madeline walks to the police car, where Massimo sits humming, and climbs inside. The car pulls away, and Madeline goes. Without waving. Without looking back.

That can't be the end of it, thinks Stefano, swigging and spilling his wine.

But he is wrong.

IX. Finale
The knife of your love

— one —

It is not shame he feels, but rather a gentle self-pity, as if he were his own child for whom he wished — but was unable to provide — a better life. Massimo wakes in his bed, next to Madeline's pleasantly hot skin, and looks about him as if for the first time: The gray cinderblocks of the building, the gray terrace, the gray twigs, the gray birds, the endless gray sky... Gray gray gray.

But the woman with gray eyes does not care. Or else she does not see the desolation, so intent is she on her imminent future. She nuzzles his chest, throws a leg over his legs, reaches for his cock.

Madeline sits in the white bathtub for nearly an hour, until the water cools and the throbbing between her thighs subsides. When she thinks of Massimo inside her she wants him inside her again, though she has already had him inside her half the night and most of the morning. She chooses not to consider, will not possibly consider why this is still not enough — why her body needs, needs specifically Massimo — so close as she now is to finding Gustavo.

She slips beneath the water into silence. An image of Gustavo flashes in her periphery, and she can smell him: scent like leaves like life that does not cause her rage to bloat. On the contrary, it shrinks, narrows to a crevice through which she cannot pass, though sunlight beckons from the other side.

Massimo pours himself a glass of orange juice and drinks it down and then stands for a moment in front of the refrigerator upon which a postcard of Miami Beach, Florida is gripped beneath a magnet shaped like the Statue of Liberty.

Liberty. *Libertà!* The imaginable freedom of possibilities.

"Take me to the train station," Madeline demands the moment she steps out of the bathroom. Scrubbed clean, refreshed, a bit of color applied to her lips, flicker of hope in her eyes…She is lovely and Massimo is astonished by her loveliness – so much the opposite of gray, though her eyes match perfectly this gray sky above this gray pitiable suburb, yet he knows the difference. His body hums with desire.

"Il treno," she insists, throwing her duffel bag over her shoulder. *"Stazione.* I want to go there now. *Ora."*

"Okay," says Massimo, pleased with his mastery of this one American word.

Before they leave, Massimo picks up the jar and shows Madeline the chrysalis inside: Through the nearly transparent sheath, a dull brown caterpillar shifts toward gold.

The air inside the train station feels colder than the air outside, though the station bustles with people arriving and departing, waiting and vending, laughing and weeping. The train from Paris via Milan is on schedule. Madeline looks at the big clock behind the ticket counter: twenty-five minutes until Clifford Beale's arrival, until what must inevitably be the beginning of the end.

She turns to Massimo who – momentarily stripped of his uniform, in loose woolen trousers and loose woolen sweater and loose woolen coat, the sensation of Madeline's lips still on his skin – feels distinctly handsome and grins about him as if the world too had suddenly metamorphosed into a place where only happy endings were possible. Ah, *sí, sí, sí. Libertà!*

But his optimism is short-lived.

"Ciao," Madeline says, wanting but unable to look him in his black eyes.

"Ciao?" Massimo asks, cocking his head to one side, still smiling, for his body does not yet comprehend what his mind already dreads.

"Sí, ciao," Madeline repeats, then turns her back to him and mumbles, "And *grazie."*

His smile collapses. He feels as if he is tumbling backward into an abyss, thus his urge is to grab her, envelope her, draw her inside him as she draws him inside her. But he does not act on his impulse. Instead, he reaches a hand toward her hair which he tentatively touches then strokes once, stammering, "Woman of the gray eyes…?" He buries his face in her hair and notes in an oddly objective fashion how its fragrance dictates that it is a woman's hair, could be none other than a woman's, and more precisely Madeline's, so familiar he is by now with her body's perfume.

The heat of your touch.

Madeline raises one hand in a flat wave: *"Ciao, Massimo."*

The noise of the station swells, fills his head with its music loud and cacophonous, and the world now looks macabre, a ridiculous dance toward death: Borrowed skin shrunk so tight in the groin he must scream. And so he does, though his agony is silent:

The knife of your love!

He turns and goes stiffly toward the exit.

Though Madeline requires indifference, she feels him go: The air dank now. Colder.

– two –

Cliff. Clifford. Clifford Beale sees Madeline long before she sees him. And he pauses in his hiddenness to
look at her, study her, compare the reality with his
vision of her to be sure it will all be worthwhile – the
purchase worth the price of the crime. No, no, he must
not think of Madeline in those terms. He loves her, of
course. Has loved her from the beginning. Quite
certain of his love and of his ability to replace that gray
unhappiness in her eyes with joy, ecstasy, gratefulness
to be alive.

Looking at her, yes, he is grateful to be alive. Not
the price of the crime but the wage.

He grins and steps away from the train and onto the
platform.

Massimo sits inside his police car in the parking lot.
The still-warm engine ticks. Sunlight glints off the
hood. Inside, a tiny bee buzzes against the windshield.
Outside, travelers weave around the car like bees:
hurried, purposeful, fleeing, returning, fleeing, taking
flight for granted. Massimo takes nothing for granted:
not flight, not sunlight, not Madeline.

He looks down at his nice wool sweater, his nice
wool trousers. Looks at his nice Italian face in the
rearview mirror. Takes nothing for granted. The bee
pummels itself against the glass. *How did it arrive at this
singular spot of the world, and what triggered its late-season
birth?* He cups a hand over the insect and folds his
palm. Its sting is modest but precise. He rolls down the
window, sticks his hand out and releases the bee. It
escapes into sunlight.

Clifford's tongue slips past Madeline's teeth and dives with a desperation that causes Madeline to gag.

"I'm sorry," he says, face bruised with desire and shame.

Madeline absently wipes her mouth.

"I've missed you," he adds – an excuse. "It's been months."

"A month and a half," says Madeline. "Precisely six weeks. Forty-two days."

Clifford nods, for he can think of nothing to say. He stares at the train that brought him here, as if to place himself more securely in the moment.

Madeline says, "Let's get something to eat." It is not so much kindness that causes her to gently take his arm and squeeze it and lead him out of the station, but knowledge that he is her only connection to Gustavo, her only hope of avoiding a life without: without music, without love, without hope. She straightens her spine, squeezes Clifford's arm and smiles up at him: Smile like a warm rain spilling over Clifford whose heart pounds in reply.

Massimo's heart pounds upon seeing Madeline and Clifford walk out of the station arm and arm, seeming happy or at least content. It is like a dream, a bad dream wherein the characters are the wrong characters, the place the wrong place, the events indecipherable. Her husband is not what he expected: too thin, too young, not so much homely as indistinguishable. What did he expect? Well, someone like himself, but cruel.

He smells his hand where Madeline's scent – vestige of reality – lingers still and concludes it is of course a bad dream from which he will eventually wake to find her hot skin against his. Meanwhile, he sleepwalks.

Madeline cannot even wait until the meal is over before asking: "How will you kill him?"

"I?" laughs Clifford. "I will not kill him."

"Surely you don't expect me – "

"No, of course not." Clifford sobers, wipes a bit of tomato sauce from his mouth. "We'll hire someone to kill him for us...for you."

Madeline frowns. "Hire someone?"

"Do you want Gustavo's blood on your hands?" Clifford snaps, not waiting for an answer. "Well, neither do I. I don't."

Madeline studies him, the lines in his face that were not there two months ago, the pinch of his mouth, the slight but discernible trembling of his hands. She leans across the table and lays her hands flat over his. "Whether we do it ourselves or not, Gustavo's blood will be on our hands. You understand this, don't you, Cliff? Our hands will be bloody from intent."

Clifford smiles wanly and rips a piece of bread in half. "Of course I understand."

Massimo sleepwalks up the stone steps of the hotel into which Madeline and Clifford have disappeared. Sleepwalks through the small tidy lobby smelling of lemons and disinfectant. Sleepwalks up to the hotel clerk who smiles at his nice Italian face until he flashes his police badge at her, whereupon she reshapes her face into one of deference. She shows Massimo the names in the register: *Herr & Frau H. Schwieger.* She insists they are German, she could tell by the man's accent.

"And the woman," Massimo asks, talking in his sleep, "Frau Schwieger, was she German as well?"

"She never spoke, but she looked German. The bones of her face. Those gray eyes."

Massimo nods sadly: "Ah, *sí, sí, sí.*"

Before going he asks to use the bathroom.

He stands over the toilet, feverish, stomach knotted, hands shaking as they unzip his trousers. He pees. He knows: Somewhere above his head is an American woman who cannot forget him masquerading as a German woman who can.

"Who is she?" asks Madeline.

Clifford hesitates. Lights a cigarette. Inhales. Exhales.

"What's her name, Cliff? Tell me."

"I don't know."

"But you've seen her."

Again he hesitates.

"Tell me!"

"No, I haven't."

"Haven't seen her?"

"That's right."

"But you're positive Gustavo's not alone."

He stares at the tip of his cigarette, looks out the window, looks at the bad painting on the wall, looks anywhere but at Madeline when he nods and says: "Gustavo is not alone."

Although it is the last thing on her mind, the last thing her body requires, Madeline climbs into bed with Clifford. She tries to imagine it is Massimo between her legs, but the shape and weight are not the same. Nor the scent.

Afterward Clifford names each city, province and country in which he searched for Gustavo, while Madeline drifts into a dreamless sleep.

Paulo shakes his head dolefully. "Massimo, Massimo. You do not even speak the same language as Signora Rivera."

Massimo shrugs. "We want the same things: love, beauty, a place without winter."

"How can you know this?"

Massimo twice slaps a big hand against his chest, over his heart.

Paulo sighs. He looks at his friend. "You are a policeman, Massimo. Here, in Bagno di Tristezza. This is your life."

"This life was a mistake."

"God does not make mistakes."

"Then why do we need policemen?"

Madeline studies the neat piles of paper on the floor. "What the hell is all this?"

"Receipts," says Clifford.

"For what?"

"My expenses."

Madeline stares, irritated by his presence. "That really wasn't necessary," and she can feel the features of her face shifting toward disgust and so pretends to have something in her eye.

"I want you to trust me," says Clifford, "my intentions. I'm not after your money. I'm not Gustavo."

"No. You're not." And before there is time for the implications of that remark to sink in she adds, "I want to be on a train for Paris by tomorrow. Is that possible?"

183

"It's possible," says Clifford, and he goes back to sorting receipts.

Young men gather in the alley behind the train station. They pick pockets, bump and snatch, wield knives with points sharp as needles. They are criminals, yeggs: small-time thugs looking to become big-time thugs. Poor and ignorant, some outright stupid, they all have one dream: to score big so they can disappear into the Italian countryside or, better yet, into America where their big money will buy them women and cars and three-piece suits and perhaps even a role in a Hollywood movie. (Perspicacity does not come easy for young ignorant thugs.)

"They're everywhere," says Clifford, "at every train station in every city in Europe. I learned to pick them out before they picked me out. Today they'll lift a few wallets, maybe run off with some luggage. But tonight, that's when they'll really go to work. Tonight the knives will come out, and the seriously ambitious will move one step closer to their idea of success." He pauses to light Madeline's cigarette, then his own. "But you have to know the difference between ambition and desperation. The desperate criminal, the one who has nothing to lose, his judgment is impaired. There's always a part of him that wants to die, that thinks death is preferable to life. He's fearless but has no self-preservation. As a result, he can't be trusted, he's dangerous. He'll make stupid mistakes because he doesn't care enough about living to think things through to their ultimate consequence. A good criminal, on the other hand, wants to live and someday live well. He may still be an animal, but he's an animal with his survival instinct intact, and his particular brand of fearlessness is motivated by a life wish, not a death wish. Therefore, when dealing with this guy everything's negotiable, and that's what we want. Room for negotiation." Clifford raps twice on the table and then smugly sits back in his chair.

Madeline blows a stream of smoke over his head. "Was that your dissertation on the criminal mind?"

Clifford laughs, then sobers when Madeline's expression remains flat.

"You realize," she says, tamping out her cigarette, "I have to trust you completely, trust your judgment."

"Yes," Clifford replies, "you do."

And then night. Black Italian night. Moonless, starless, rain piercing the blackness wet and slick. Trains do not stop running because of rain or blackness, nor do travelers stop traveling. Thus, the alley behind the train station is not empty even on this black wet night – although the ones who brave it are, as Clifford would say, seriously ambitious.

Clifford swallows a third shot of grappa and stands. "Wait here."

"I want to go with you."

He shakes his head, to which the grappa has gone, and sways.

"Why not?"

"You don't speak Italian," he says, pulling his baseball cap low over his brow, "and you'd only distract them." He smiles a smile so wrought with anxiety that his whole face twitches from the effort. "It's like a movie, isn't it?"

"No, it isn't."

"You're right," he says, "you're right. This is real. It's real." And after a pause, he awkwardly bends to kiss Madeline on the mouth but misses his mark, and his wet lips graze her nose, kiss a corner of her upper lip. Another hesitation and then he spins around and exits the cafe.

Madeline catches sight of him through the window, standing beneath the blue awning, trying again and again to light a cigarette, finally succeeding, then smoking a while, hunched inside his blue coat as if this were a cold Midwestern winter, which it is not, though it is winter and not at all warm, and suddenly he is gone into the black wet darkness. And it is then that Madeline sees her reflection in the window, hears in her head the words faint and fleeting, yet unmistakable: *What have you done?*

But it is too late, of course. It was too late yesterday and the day before that and the day before that…. A thing is set in motion, and the motion becomes the catalyst that transforms the thing into another thing and yet another by the exponential speed that it travels.

Massimo understands this. He is a policeman, after all. He has scraped up the mess when a thing out of control collides, inevitably collides with the living.

But no more scraping, he thinks as he watches Clifford cross the street to the alley behind the train station. Then he turns to gaze at Madeline who sits alone at a table in a small dirty cafe, running her hands through her hair again and again in time with the music – a simple Italian ballad – which she does not even hear.

– three –

"It is like death," Gustavo said when they had reached the apex. "Or maybe it is like a place between to live and to die?"

Madeline nodded. A place between. Yes.

All around them the land lay obscured beneath a dense fog, a white fog more like smoke than vapor. Entirely obscured except for a nearby tree that stood before them – solitary birch tree, leafless, its papery bark peeled away like dead flesh from bone, and the bone bleached white by the sun, so that when the fog rose, invariably rose from the river, it was all white everywhere they looked, and white even beyond the birch that grew on the edge of a precipice overlooking the river basin filled to the brim with fog so dense Madeline believed she could step past the birch and off the precipice and keep on walking straight into her next incarnation. But she would want the same life, wouldn't she? In fact, the same moment: Gustavo beside her on this white plateau above the river, her hand in his, his scent mixed with hers – moment eternal, like their love. She believed.

Gustavo stroked his cheek against the smooth white trunk of the birch. "I think it is true. When we walk out of this fog, our life will be behind us, in a place that we can not to return."

"And then?" she asked.

He bit her neck and growled: "Death."

"And after death?"

"Salvation," Gustavo said without hesitation.

"You believe that?"

"Sure," he laughed and kissed her. "Why not!"

Fog like a cataract on the eye of the world, and the train rumbling through the cataract, and Madeline inside the train, staring out at the fog, at the present, at nothing, at the place between dying and living.

"Do you believe in life after death?" she asks.

Clifford looks up from his magazine. "I don't know, I don't think about it."

"Why not?"

"Because thinking about it won't change the results."

"What if you're wrong. What if our preconceptions of the afterlife give it its shape."

He closes the magazine. "Are you having second thoughts about all this?"

She looks out the window and lies: "No."

He leans forward to draw a finger across her knee. She pinches her eyes shut. He slumps back. After a while, she sighs:

"I want to paint again."

Still wounded, Clifford snorts, "That's your idea of an afterlife?"

"It's part of it."

"And the other part?"

"Music."

"Music?"

"Somehow."

"What kind of music?"

All music, she thinks, *all music that is and is not music, that makes living bearable, at times even enjoyable: bow on the strings, fingers on the keys, lips to the ear, sigh between the breasts, laughter and song and whisper...*

"What kind?" Clifford repeats.

She looks at him, eyes hard: "Never mind."

She gets up and leaves the compartment. The train sways back and forth in the whiteness. She walks along the corridor with no destination except escape, but the train moves inexorably forward and the whiteness dissolves in lacunae of color, the dry faded spent hues of winter.

The afterlife: a place without winter.

So we are still dead, thinks Massimo, staring through the train window, watching the blurred winter landscape break through the fog. He looks up the word, *nebbia*, in his Italian-English dictionary and says aloud, "Fog," once, twice, three times.

Two plump women seated across from him whisper and giggle. They glance up at his nice Italian face wrought now with melancholia and perhaps also doubt: that he has acted impulsively, unwisely even. He pulls the jar out of his knapsack and holds it up to the window where the sun is now beginning to shine through a dirty yellow haze. The women stare at the chrysalis, entranced by its delicacy. Pleased by their appreciation of beautiful possibilities, Massimo taps a finger on the jar to move the twig to a position more advantageous for viewing, and he grins at the plump women while explaining the transformation taking place inside the transparent world. And as he leans forward, offering the jar for closer inspection, he sees – with a vision more accurate than peripheral, that has nothing to do with the eyes – sees Madeline glide past like a ghost out of his future.

"Madeline Rivera."

She halts upon hearing her name spoken so softly she cannot be sure she has heard it at all. So familiar, the voice, she is certain she will turn to see Gustavo. And for a moment she does see him: black hair, black eyes, white white teeth inside soft lips...

"*Mi dispiace...*" is all Massimo can think to say. To apologize – *for what?* he silently asks, loathing his lack of resolve here, now, at this important moment. *But they are all important, of course – places, moments where our lives correspond.*

She goes to him. "What are you doing here?"

Even if he could understand the question he could not respond in a way to make her understand his answer. Thus they stand in silence, swaying side to side in unison, longing with mathematical predictability to smell upon the other's skin that private unnamable odor.

He repeats, "Madeline Rivera," as if the weight of her name on his lips will convey the weight upon his heart. The train lurches. They stumble. He grabs her around the waist and draws her to him for a moment – brief moment long enough for Madeline to feel his erection against her belly, and to wonder briefly in that brief moment where they might go to kiss and grope – until the moment is ended by Clifford who appears behind Massimo's left shoulder, eyebrows knit with insult and perhaps dread that he might have to rescue Madeline, fight a man whose bulk makes him the odds-on favorite, and he, Clifford, is not good at fighting, was never good, having fought only twice in his life and lost both times, miserably defeated but made wise enough to thereafter avoid fighting if at all possible, and so wondering now, *Is it at all possible?* before he asks in a voice loud but wavering, "Madeline, are you all right?"

Madeline says quickly to Massimo, "Excuse me," as he says quickly to her, *"Scusatemi,"* and releases her, and lets her pass.

The moment is over. But no one will forget. Certainly not Clifford.

"Who the hell was that guy?" he asks, bravely, now that Massimo has disappeared into another car.

"I have no idea," replies Madeline calmly, though her heart is a hammer.

"He had his hands on you."

"The train swerved," she says. "He kept me from falling."

"Oh, *right.* Fucking horny Italians."

Massimo – fucking horny Italian – walks to the last car, turns around and begins walking back: head down, heart torn, cock hard.

The door to a toilet opens and a small wiry youth dressed in cheap denim and dirty boots with heels worn to the nails, hair slicked back from his low pimpled brow, mustache like a thin smudge of soot, gold chain at his neck, gold watch on one wrist, gold rings on three fingers, steps out still buttoning the fly of his cheap denim jeans and runs headlong into Massimo – his head, in fact, butting Massimo's chest – and he says in Italian, "Hey, fuck!" just as Massimo says in Italian, "Excuse me." And the youth, the yegg, the small-time thug glimpses Massimo's profile before it disappears into the next car, and a flash of recognition awakens in his sleepy thug-brain, and he pulls from the pocket of his cheap denim jacket photos already worn from nearly ceaseless scrutiny, and thinks with his mind that is ignorant and dull but not entirely stupid: *Gustavo Rivera!* – never thinking far enough to form the question, *Why would Gustavo Rivera be on a train bound for Paris if he's already in Paris?* and so congratulating himself on his deductive abilities as he tucks the photos back into his pocket.

He returns to his seat, winks at the pretty adolescent girl across the aisle, looks out at the blurred landscape, sunny now and as gold as his front tooth that catches the sun and reflects it onto the palm of his hand that he holds open in order to display the golden light to the girl who stares in timid wonder as he closes his hand and the light disappears, opens his hand and the light reappears. Closes. Opens. Light coming and going. He plays this game until the girl grows tired of wonderment, simply tired, and leans against her mother and closes her eyes.

He opens his palm, grins, and the light appears. He too stares in wonder: *Gold in the hand,* he thinks, folding his palm, closing his mouth, vanishing the light. Because he is on a train bound for Paris, he believes he has already arrived.

– four –

And then Paris. Wet-veiled and aloof. Pale wash of thinned ink…Yes, yes, yes, all that. But also this: silence lurking at the edges, waiting to debut.

Gustavo senses it even in the safety of the rehearsal hall: there, just beyond the light's reach, and there in the darkened wings, and there too in the tattered red velvet seats hidden by darkness. Silence malicious and obese, a jealous critic anticipating the misplaced note.

But there is no misplaced note. Gustavo plays with a perfection that surprises even him, though he keeps his surprise to himself lest other members of the chamber orchestra doubt his skill. He cannot afford their doubt, nor his own: He knows his seat in the orchestra is tentative, a favor to the director's old friend, Bernard Allande. This is another country, another life, and it is a good life full of possibilities such as a hand upon a bow upon the strings moving without flaw, and he is amazed: *Mi dios, mon dieu, my god, it is good to be alive!*

Rehearsal ends. Musicians pack up their instruments and begin leaving. The viola player bends down to whisper an invitation. She is attractive enough, he thinks, but he smiles, *"Non, merci,"* and she pulls down her mouth in a good-natured pout and leaves. The director pats Gustavo on the back, invites him to dinner, but Gustavo declines, saying he wishes to practice a while longer. The director nods and grins, impressed with Gustavo's dedication.

But it is not dedication, it is fear. Fear of the encroaching silence – not here, perhaps, but somewhere, somewhere. *Una vida sin musica.*

He settles the violin under his chin, lays the bow upon the strings, light as a feather upon stone.

¿Que es...que es...? The violin sings the beginning strains of an adagio that does not exist except in Gustavo's head, and there only vaguely. (The caprice now is complete: notes committed to the page.) Beautiful adagio. Safeguard against the encroaching silence.

He rests the violin on his left knee, touches the tip of the bow to the wooden stage, taps it once, twice, looks out at an audience that does not exist, enveloped in darkness that does. He listens for a minute, two minutes, three, five, ten, thirteen.

¿Que es una vida sin musica?

This, he thinks, *this.*

Silence clawing.

Fear spilling over.

He puts away his violin and heads to a bar near the Gare du Nord where the prostitutes are clean enough and reasonably priced.

The train pulls into the Gare du Nord four minutes late. If it had arrived on schedule, they would have passed each other in the street, Gustavo and Madeline, and everything would have been, might have been different. *If, if, if.* The train was four minutes late and there is nothing that can be done about it now. What is the point of speculating on events that do not, will not, cannot exist because the one moment shaped specifically for their occurrence was misplaced?

Thus:

Fast forward.

It is what they are all thinking: Madeline, Clifford, Massimo, yegg. They all wish to fast forward, to be in the moment after: after the crime, after winter, after the fifty thousand Deutsche marks have been changed to lire, after what's unknown is known and this country this life is a stopover nearly forgotten, residue, like a nightmare whose images dissolve with morning and all that remains is a discomfiting sensation, like indigestion that will soon enough go away, inevitably go away like the past.

But they can only move this far forward and then this far, toward L'Hotel Finale, for things have been planned in advance, orchestrated with such amazing deftness that one step too far forward will cause it all to fall completely, disastrously, irreparably apart.

Mother may I? Clifford thinks, grinning, for it is he who has orchestrated this *danse macabre*, and therefore omnipotently believes it is he who controls the dancers. "No you may not," he orders Madeline, loudly, gaily.

"What?" she asks, distracted, touching first her hair, then her lips, glancing over her shoulder in search of Massimo who trails at a discreet distance.

"Oh, nothing!" Clifford sings. He kisses Madeline on the cheek with a loud wet smack.

Madeline squints at him. It's his sudden smugness she loathes, isn't it? Or is it perhaps his callousness. After all, they are going to kill a man, and Clifford seems happy – no, gleeful about it.

Dear Gustavo: And why am I not happy about it, gleeful? After so much waiting, why am I not simply intoxicated with joy?

Clifford hums a pleasant Sousa march, bobs his head in time to the music, sets their luggage down at the front desk.

Or is it that she feels morally, ethically, sexually obliged to Clifford and therefore resents him with a loathing that seems now to outstrip her rage against Gustavo? "I want a separate room," she says.

Clifford stops humming. He drops his jaw, then clamps it shut, teeth gnashing.

"Try to understand," she pleads. "Put yourself in my place and try to understand."

He takes her roughly by the arm and pulls her into a corner of the lobby and leans in close, so close she can smell the apple he ate on the walk from the train station. "I *have* put myself in your place," he whispers, pinching her arm tight, "that's why I'm here. In fact, that's why *you're* here, Madeline. I've done all the legwork, all the planning, all the searching and finding and plotting. I've taken enormous risks, risks and precautions you can't imagine, precautions the police will never imagine. I've done all of this for you, damn it! For *you*. And what, I ask, what what *what* in hell have you done for me?"

She stares at his hand on her arm until he removes it, then stares at his face, precisely: stares into his eyes which are full of fury but no fury great enough to defend him from Madeline's fat fat rage: "Would you like me to suck your cock, Cliff? Let you come on my tits? In my face?"

He looks at her in horror and tries to back away but is stopped by the wall against his spine. She closes in, backing him into a corner both literal and figurative.

"Or fuck me until I can't walk?" she persists. "Is that what you want, Cliff? Would that suffice as payment for all you've done, as you say, for me, damn it, for *me*?"

196

His face burns red and he wants to flee. But he is not fifteen anymore, though that is exactly how young he feels: ashamed of what he said, ashamed of what she said, ashamed of who they are and what they are doing and where they will, he is certain, end up if things continue to occur as they are not meant to occur: disorderly, not according to plan. And so he relents: "I'm sorry, I'm sorry, that's not what I meant, I just meant…"

But, of course, that is more or less what he meant and there is no way around it and there is no lie that will make Madeline believe otherwise. The silence between them, around them in the dingy hotel, is deafening, but the Sousa march absurdly continues on inside Clifford's head as if music exists separate from the listener, rehearsing itself over and over without end while the listener passes through it on his way to another melody. Or, in Madeline's case, another silence, which is all she hears: no Sousa march for her.

"Please," Madeline says, taking his hands in hers, whispering with feigned tenderness: "Understand."

"I do," he says, though he doesn't. Nevertheless, he takes a separate room down the hall in #402.

It is a cheap hotel, small but clean enough, off the beaten path, as the guidebooks would say. But it is not in the guidebooks, though the owners have tried to get a listing each of the three years it has been open. It is racism, they are sure, they are Pakistanis, and it is true Parisians are not fond of Pakistanis or any foreigner who will take Parisian jobs away from Parisians, certainly not in this economy. And now they are wondering if in fact their efforts have proved fruitful because now there are four new guests all in the same day: one

German couple and two unrelated Italians – though the one, the young dirty one, is not exactly the type of guest they would prefer. But this close to bankruptcy, how can they complain?

And so they are smiling, and their cousin who speaks no English and only a few words of French has something to do besides clean up after the prostitutes, male and female, whose business has kept them in business these three years.

"Cousin!" one of the owners calls in Punjabi, and the cousin hurries over to the front desk, beaming. The owner hands him a fat envelope sealed with red wax and an imprint of a German crest and states slowly, carefully, as if reciting: "Deliver this to Room 112. Do not attempt to open it, do not attempt to look inside. Personally deliver it to the guest, and make sure it is the right guest."

"But how will I know it is the right guest?" asks the cousin.

"Room 112 is an Italian man," the owner says with no patience, "short, skinny, not clean. And right here," says the owner, tapping his left front tooth, "gold."

The short skinny unclean Italian with the gold front tooth tosses his grimy backpack onto the bed and snorts at the coverlet which is thin and cheap and flocked with daisies and so is offensive, he thinks, insulting to a criminal of his caliber, he thinks, mistaking the invitation to the crime for the crime itself. He considers, while scowling down at the coverlet, how it will feel to fast-forward and finally kill a man. Particularly a man this beautiful, he thinks, extracting the photos of Gustavo from his pocket, studying them once more before sealing them in a blue envelope. A man with such white white teeth, with wealth and health and enemies – how admirable to have such serious and determined enemies! A man who is everything that he, the yegg, is not and so deserves to die, of course, deserves the black fire of the knife sinking into such beautiful flesh.

"Uhn!" he whispers violently, violently jabbing his knife into the air in front of him and twisting it, once to the left, once to the right, then "Uhn!" he whispers again as he repeats each move.

Sure, it will feel good, he concludes, methodically wiping his clean knife blade against his dirty denim jacket, good to kill a man whose excessive good fortune makes him excessively deserving of death – the fortunate have to pay somehow, don't they, it's only fair. And besides, there is money to be made, and the point of money is to relieve all possibility of remorse, isn't it?

Satisfied, he grins and tucks the knife back inside his shirtsleeve. He goes to the window and yanks open the plain muslin curtains and looks out at the gloomy alley and then directly across at a building nearly identical to the one in which he now stands frowning through sooty window panes. He expected a view, and is offended – twice now offended, temper rising – that there is no view, but he will have a view, goddamn it, even if he has to create one himself. He unlatches the window and pulls, then pushes, pulling harder and pushing harder each time, but the window will not open. He runs his fingers around the chipped paint of the frame and realizes the window has been nailed shut. He slams his fist against the glass, hard enough to jar loose the old gray dried caulking that crumbles onto his head. He tries to slap it away but only breaks it into smaller pieces that get tangled in his greasy hair. He plucks out the pieces gingerly, with disgust, as if they were bird shit, and before he has finished plucking them out, there is a knock at the door, and he takes determined strides as if expecting someone and opens the door to find the Pakistani cousin standing at attention like a soldier, the red-sealed envelope pressed tightly to his chest.

The yegg snatches the envelope out of the Pakistani's hands, shoves the blue envelope into them, mumbles, *"Grazie,"* and slams the door.

The Pakistani cousin stands helpless a full minute, trying to decide what to do next. First, he does not know what to do with the blue envelope. Second, he does not feel he is certain that the Italian man – a boy, really – is the right Italian, though he was indeed short and skinny and appeared unclean, in fact smelling quite bad, like soured cabbage.

He knocks again. Waits. Knocks louder. The door opens and the yegg stands scowling before him, mouth pinched tight in irritation.

"Pardonnez-moi," says the Pakistani cousin, *"mais je suis...,"* and that is virtually the extent of his French. Not that fluency would matter since the yegg speaks no French at all and speaks his own language badly. The cousin holds up the blue envelope and offers the yegg his most convincing expression of perplexity. The yegg emphatically points at the room number written on the envelope – Room 402 – then points down the hall toward the elevator, points at the room number, then at the elevator, room number, elevator, until finally the Pakistani says, "Ah-h-h!" and nods.

The yegg slams the door in his face.

The problem of the gold tooth.

The Pakistani knocks again. Waits. Raises his fist to knock again when the yegg opens the door with such force that a wind is created that lifts his greasy hair from his forehead.

The Pakistani cousin smiles brightly, broadly, showing his big white teeth, hoping the yegg will return the gesture out of sympathy or reflex and thus reveal the gold tooth, but the yegg only stares dumbly as before, lips tight, and scratches his ass. An awkward silence ensues in which the cousin, in his discomfort, grasps at the one thing that always brings him solace: music, in particular the music of home and, more particular, of his neighborhood in Lahore where a lovely boy with sad eyes and long thin fingers would play a *sarangi* and sing on the street corner every evening in hopes that someone of wealth and discriminating taste would discover him and take him home and feed him and clothe him and make him the most famous singer in all of Pakistan, when in reality it was merely the Pakistani cousin and those like him who would discover the lovely boy night after night only to give him paltry amounts of money to follow them down an alley and perform fallatio on them or, in the cousin's case, perform fallatio on the boy – so adorable was he, his cock as lovely as his fingers – and afterward the boy returning to the same street corner with the same miraculously unsullied dream...*that* music, which the Pakistani cousin now recalls with glazed eyes and a nostalgic, idiotic smile.

The yegg, in his own idiotic fashion, misinterprets and reaches into his back pocket and pulls out a thousand lire note which he hands to the cousin, then slams the door.

The problem of the gold tooth.

Ah, well. The Pakistani cousin shrugs and tucks the lire (far less valuable than he thinks) into the breast pocket of his uniform. Gold tooth or not, this Italian is certainly short and skinny and not at all clean. Is the opposite of the other Italian guest who earlier requested hotel stationery, and there are no more Italians in the hotel, so gold tooth or not what can it matter?

The yegg slides a finger under the flap of the envelope, and the red wax seal pops off, falls to the floor, bounces under the bed. Inside the envelope are ten thousand Deutsche marks, approximately one-fifth the promised payment for the crime: the price of a beautiful life. He weighs the money, smells it, bites down on the paper with his gold tooth, grins. And so it is real, he thinks, it is happening: what he has dreamed of all nineteen years of his life. And the taste of the money reminds him he is thirsty, and the itch in his balls reminds him he is horny, so he stuffs a handful of Deutsche marks into the back pocket of his jeans and goes to find a bar where the whiskey is smooth and the prostitutes cheap and relatively clean, unlike those he frequents at home.

> M.
> I must to have you. I want that your skin to
> be upon my skin. That your...

Massimo sits upon a hotel bed covered with an exquisite quilt of indigo velvet upon which gold satin crescents lay scattered like so many moons in a starless sky. Tropical sky where the wind is a continuous slow caress, and the warm rain like wet kisses, and the scent of the earth and sea healing...

He thumbs through his Italian-English dictionary until he finds the correct word: *fragranza*. Prints its translation neatly as he can upon the simple hotel stationery. Continues:

> fragrance inside my breath. That your sigh to make inside my ear. We musts to be one persona singular. It is *il fato*, the fate, yes?
> Massimo, Room N° 310

He folds the letter, puts it in an envelope, seals it, kisses the seal. He writes across the front: *M. Rivera* — already thinking: *Madelina Benevento* — and gazes at the envelope a long while, too rapt in dreams of transformation to remember it is *Frau Schweiger* moving from one European hotel to another, not Madeline Rivera. He goes to the window to gaze across a horizon of gray tin roofs and above at a gray-veiled sky that is just now dissolving into an ordinary sunset of bloody gold, and imagines that there, beyond that distant path down which the sun now descends, another life awaits him in another country, and a woman with sorrowful gray eyes turns to him and smiles.

The owners of L'Hotel Finale celebrate what they mistakenly presume to be their long-awaited success with a fine meal of cheeseburgers and fries and two colas apiece, dining in a back room of the hotel before later indulging in a Brahms concert while their Pakistani cousin mans the front desk, grinning with excessive pride that his prosperous relatives would trust him not with their lives, no, but at least with their livelihood. Unfortunately, he does not speak French and does not speak Italian so that when Massimo hands him an envelope and says, "Please deliver this immediately," first in Italian, then in French, the Pakistani cousin only stares at the envelope and grins and stupidly shakes his head.

Massimo is about to take back the envelope in order to demonstrate what the cousin must do, when the yegg comes swaggering through the hotel lobby, swaggering from the weight of Deutsche marks in his back pocket. He slaps the marks onto the desk, demanding in Italian, "I need French money," a demand comprehensible to only Massimo who looks at the Deutsche marks, then at the yegg, then at the Deutsche marks, automatically – out of habit and bloodlines – trying to connect the dots between *German marks* and a German *Herr H. Schwieger* and this skinny Italian punk who looks vaguely familiar. And the vaguely familiar Italian punk looks at Massimo and immediately flinches, going quite pale at the nearness of what he believes is his target of gold, saying, "Rivera!" to himself, aloud, so that Massimo stops connecting dots and grins congenially and replies, "*Sí*, Rivera," and then nods at the envelope in the Pakistani cousin's hands, repeating to the cousin, "Rivera," and pointing first at the envelope then at the mail boxes behind the cousin until finally, *finally* the cousin comprehends.

And the yegg, too, comprehends – but something entirely different: that the beautiful man now walking toward the elevator – *Rivera!* – deserves to die for the overwhelming gifts God has bestowed upon him, for the meek must inherit the earth, and so Rivera will die, if all goes as planned, and he, the yegg, will have carried out God's work: *"In nomine patre, per omnia sæcula sæculorum."* He grins, making the sign of the cross in the air between them, then turns to grin and wink at the Pakistani cousin who grins and winks back, though he doesn't know why.

The elevator rises. Massimo closes his eyes, imagines another life awaiting him in another country, and a woman with sorrowful gray eyes turns to him and smiles.

But Madeline does not smile. Not now. Not yet. Not with so much still ahead until there is so much left behind. *Fast forward, fast forward.* But she cannot. She looks out at the descending sunset, through a window that opens onto the winter air of Paris where she imagines a man, once her husband, living out the last moments of his life...

fucking a French whore who is so thin and wan – a pale dry reed – he fears he will break her in two with each thrust of his cock, and he thrusts hard, harder, trying hard to come in this cheap hotel room where there is no fucking mirror, no mirror to watch himself fucking, telling himself it is the lack of mirror, the thickness of condom that prevents his orgasm, knowing full well how worn these lies have become.

It's true: A man this beautiful could have virtually any woman in Paris, yet he fucks an emaciated whore in the cheapest room of a cheap hotel run by Pakistanis who smile far too much, fucks her because she demands nothing of him but one hundred francs per hour for this: one of the possibilities of a freedom no longer sudden.

A man this beautiful trying hard to come, imagining the whore to be anyone but who she is – an Asian flutist, for example, or African princess, South Ameri-

can pygmy, robot of platinum, doe caught in brambles
...anyone, anything in order to arouse him to ejacula-
tion. And the emaciated whore begins to wince now
with every dry thrust, the smell of hot latex and her
own bruised blood filling her nostrils as she fills his
ears with what she believes to be sexy words, looking
at her watch, wincing, digging her soft red nails into
his back, not from ecstasy, of course, but from pain –
her own and that which she hopes to inflict upon him,
this beautiful man whom she loathes for his beauty and
his sexual incompetence, this beautiful rich man who
thrusts his blue-bruised cock and pinches his eyes shut
and imagines the exotic and the unreal and the per-
verse until somewhere, perhaps down the hall, a bell
rings, fragile and familiar, and he involuntarily imagines – Pavlovian reaction – imagines it is Madeline
beneath him, smells the faint delicate scent of her sweat
and sex on a morning in spring with a breeze blowing
across the yellow bed in the yellow bedroom, and the
ringing of the fragile bell, and the gratitude in her gray
eyes, and her weeping as she came and came again,
coming and weeping and whispering indistinguishable
words over and over, and he coming deep inside her
(as he now comes inside the condom inside the whore),
and that moment after, just before he would roll off
Maddi and lay at her side (as he now rolls off the
whore but rolls further still so that he no longer must
feel her or smell her), that sweet moment after, when
they would bury their heads in each other's neck and
think of nothing, nothing, nothing: tender moment
after when everything ceased to exist, no longer required, because the body had been sated and the soul,
it seemed, well fed.

Nothing.

Which is not what he thinks of now, for he is disturbed, in fact, furious that it was Madeline's face, the memory of her hands and cunt and tears, that finally brought him to orgasm. Asks himself: *What does it mean except that I am deranged, deranged to covet – if only fleetingly and for practical purposes – covet my wife?* Mi dios, mon dieu, *my god, what but my own madness?* For it cannot be that he loves Madeline, for he never loved her, did he? Did he? *Did he?*

Gustavo sat in the stiff wooden chair, the only chair in the room of his apartment, playing Mahler for her, an adagietto because it seemed to suit so well her disposition: sad, sweet, her voice flowing slow as honey, like her tears. And, yes, it's true Maddi had wept, and he loved that the music caused her to weep, and he loved that when he made love to her she wept again, a weeping full of such sweetness that he had to ask, "But now where is the music?" and Maddi, Madeline, his wife-to-be pointed at her heart beneath her pretty breasts and replied, still weeping, "It is here." And, all right, yes, he loved those things then, there, in another life another country, but that does not mean he loved Madeline, does it? *Does it?*

"No!" he cries, bolting upright, scaring the emaciated whore half to death, which is not far since she is half dead already. He leaps up from the bed and paces the room. Halts to stare through the iron grille barring the sooty window, at the black-cloaked alley beyond – in effect, staring at nothing, though it is not the same nothing as in the moment after. A minute passes. Two…three…five. *Una vida sin…que?*

He turns and glances about the small darkening room as if searching for someone who should be there, whose presence is expected but so taken for granted that it is only its absence that recalls it at all. His eyes settle upon his violin case. He picks it up and sits naked in the wooden chair near the door. He takes out the violin.

The whore who has been watching Gustavo with a suspicion typical of bruised whores sees this as her cue to take the money and go while the night is only now coming on and there are so many men and women waiting to be serviced yet.

Gustavo draws a single note from a single string, stretching it long to fill the terrible silence of the room.

The whore, dressed now in her pleasant yellow dress, slinks toward the door. Gustavo grabs her wrist and says, "Stay!" She looks at him without comprehending until he repeats the demand in French: *"Restez!"* She shakes her head no, taps on her watch. He holds up one finger to keep her in place while he fishes a hundred francs from his wallet, hands them to her, motions her to sit on the floor at his feet. She looks at the cold stone floor, then at the hundred francs, then again at the floor, shakes her head no. He gives her another hundred. She shrugs and sits on the cold stone floor, hard beneath her bony ass, and pretends to be attentive – though she is already bored when he settles the violin beneath his chin and beings to play.

And so it is:

In every room of L'Hotel Finale, movement stops where there is movement. Where there is breathing, breathing stops. Where there is a woman who weeps at all things beautiful, there is weeping. And where there is a man who knows but cannot cannot cannot admit that a life without music is the same as a life without love is the same as a life without, there is music:

¿Que es... que es... que es una vida sin...?

And the memory of music. And the silence that sits hunched at the edge of everything.

– five –

A caterpillar disappears into the dust of new wings. Wings of gold and black. Black eyes like glass beads, astonished by the world to come. Transformation and unfolding so complete that not even the caterpillar's ghost will remember itself or its old life among the grasses and dank earth and flooding rains. Forget all and be glad about it: wings spread toward the sun.

Sole, mare, sale degli amanti...

Sun, sea, salt of lovers...

He is certain she will come to him, just as he is certain the chrysalis will one day split from the reflex of transformation, just as he is certain he will one day shed his forgettable uniform through the knife of her love.

Madeline rings the silver bell on the front desk and notes only peripherally its fragile familiarity, for her mind is elsewhere, orchestrating the body's desire. Desire so specific it now goes by another name:

Massimo.

"Hello?" she calls, ringing again.

The Pakistani cousin, who sits on the toilet in the bathroom just off the lobby, hears the bell – once, twice, three times – and worries between the patience of his bowels and the patience of a hotel guest. Inevitably choosing his bowels that have no patience at all.

Madeline steps behind the front desk. It is immaculate: everything in its place, and the place for the guest registry in the center drawer which she opens, removing the heavy book and flipping through a hundred blank pages, back to front, until she comes upon the last page of signatures and runs her finger down the list – past the Schweigers: *Herr H.* and *Frau H.* in their respective rooms – down to *M. Benevento*, Room 310.

In her body's haste toward fulfillment, she does not notice the last signature, little more than a scrawl but legible enough to a Pakistani cousin with a letter to deliver: *M. Rivera*.

As in: *Monsieur Rivera*, deduced the Pakistani cousin.

Monsieur Gustavo Rivera who discovers on his way out of the cheap dark hotel room smelling of dust and smoke and gin and sex: an envelope slipped under the door.

> M.
> I must to have you. I want that your skin to be upon my skin. That your fragrance inside my breath. That your sigh to make inside my ear. We musts to be one persona singular. It is *il fato*, the fate, yes?
> Massimo, Room N° 310

He reads and rereads the letter, trying to summon the face behind the name. But there have been so many faces – named and nameless – women and men who have desired him for the beauty of his face, the heat of his hands, the taste of his cock. Women and men who have tried to steal from him not his money but his soul, blaming their desire, their thievery, on love when love had nothing to do with it. Thus he, Gustavo, has nothing to do with love, whenever he can help it.

He crumples the letter and throws it to the floor. He picks up his violin case. He stands a moment looking at the door, a heaviness upon his shoulders as if the possibilities of freedom had grown simply too fat to bear.

He looks at his shoes, then at the crumpled letter. He picks it up, smoothes it, folds it, tucks it in his breast pocket. He goes out into the cold Paris night.

Cold Paris night of December 18.

Scent of what's unknown and what's yet to be known: scent of blood. And the black-winged oily-winged bird of prey having already made its descent.

Night descended and feasting on the flesh of the living, pecking at Clifford Beale's living flesh – in particular, his heart. Pecking without restraint until it bleeds, his heart, bleeds into the darkened room where he sits on the blood-red bedspread, hunched over in his boxer shorts, staring at his feet which he imagines to be cloven, the feet of a devil, a demon, a monster, an incubus? In any case, the feet of a terrible creature willing to murder to gain possession of a woman who may never love him in return. Who may in fact be incapable of loving him or anyone but her husband – if even him. Who may have always been incapable and thus capable of anything. For example: betrayal.

He sits straight, attentive to the scent of something yet unknown. He leaps to his feet and begins dressing, carefully, as if for an important occasion. The rooms adjoining his are vacant so there is no one to hear and appreciate his fascinating rendition of Puccini's "Nessun Dorma!" sung like a madman, a killer to be.

Nessun dorma!

No one is sleeping!

Not the yegg drinking in a bar near the Gare du Nord, flashing his money and gold tooth, trying with Italian words to seduce an emaciated French whore in a pleasant yellow dress, as if seducing a whore were ever necessary.

Not the Pakistani cousin who remembers the poor *sarangi* player in Lahore and rubs his cock and grins.

Not Clifford who cannot decide between the blue socks and the brown.

Not Massimo who spreads Madeline's thighs and buries his face in the particular taste of her sex, wet and pink and smelling, he thinks, like some unnamed fruit, ripe and fallen. And, yes, she is fallen – broken-winged angel – into his bed, into his mouth, weeping now as she comes, and comes again as he enters her and kisses her mouth and sucks on her tongue so she can taste her own succulent juices, and he whispers: *Madelina Madelina Madelina...*

And not Madeline who disappears into the tender moment after, body sated, soul at least momentarily silenced of its eternal scream, thinking of nothing – almost. For inside the shadow of nothing squats the nagging of what remains undone.

Dear Gustavo: What remains undone is the undoing of you?

And not Gustavo, undone by memory, by the past surfacing as quiet and insidious as rats rising from the waters of the Seine that he sits alongside, smoking a cigarillo laced with hashish, listlessly kicking at the rats that creep and sniff around his violin case and shoes. Gustavo undone: gazing off at the black water, trying to think of nothing at all but thinking of everything all at once. Getting to his feet amid the squeal and scurry of rats to stand at the edge of the Seine and inspect his tired but unquestionably beautiful face. Wondering: *How cold the black water, how deep, how silent?*

Nessun dorma!

Not the Seine that flows relentlessly through night-blackened landscapes, blackened lives and histories…into its future, as ignorant of itself as of the rats and garbage and dead bodies floating in its waters.

Nessun dorma!

Not the sun toward which the world perpetually leans as if trying to convey a tantalizing secret.

Not the moon that refuses to extinguish its borrowed light, there above the eastern horizon, just before a veil of clouds descends to swallow it.

Not the sky descending, breaking apart in small crystals of ice light as the air from which they're borne, and tumbling tumbling like all things light and heavy aloft, tumbling to the earth – sparkling in the morning sun just before the veil of winter swallows them, too.

And everyone in L'Hotel Finale staring out this window or that, marveling like children at the pretty glittering air, while an older deeper decayed vision of the world is turned toward their ignorant future and this bloody bloody day.

— six —

"Where were you last night?" Clifford asks, still wearing yesterday's clothes: now rumpled oxford shirt and jeans; brown socks, not the blue.

Madeline looks out upon the veiled city. She exhales a lungful of smoke against the window, and the heat and wet of her breath form a small cloud there beneath the roiling smoke. She starts to write... *What?* She drags a finger down through the cloud, drawing a thin line significant only for its thoughtlessness. "I was here," she replies, "in my room."

"Bullshit!" Though Clifford has never raised a hand to a woman, his impulse is to strike her, shake her, force her to tell him the truth so he can forgive her, because if he cannot forgive her then how can he possibly love her, and if he can not love her then what is the point of anything?

"You weren't here," he says, thumbnail digging into the palm of his hand. "I stopped by three times last night. You weren't here."

"I was asleep."

"No," Clifford says slowly, beads of sweat breaking out above his lip, "you weren't here."

Madeline turns, tamps out her cigarette, brushes back her hair with both hands but does not complete the gesture: arms raised over her head, hands still tangled in her hair. "How do you know I wasn't here?"

"Because you weren't!" Clifford shouts, slamming his fist into the wall.

Madeline does not flinch, though she lowers her arms. "Did you come into my room, Cliff? Did you bribe the concierge to let you into my room?"

He looks at her, childlike, amazed at her acuity, then looks away. "No, of course not."

"Then you can't possibly know if I was asleep *here* or not, can you?"

He thinks: A game of checkers and he is the last red checker on the board, left with only two open squares and both of them losing moves. He smiles sickly.

She goes to the bed, sits, crosses her left ankle over her right knee and polishes a black patent shoe with the bedspread. "When will he do it?" she asks.

"It's better if you don't know."

"Today? Tomorrow?"

"Don't ask me that."

She looks at him obliquely. "Do *you* know when?"

"Of course I know."

"When?"

He wavers, eyes flitting about the room. "Tomorrow," he says.

Madeline spits on the brass buckle no longer shiny and rubs and rubs and rubs. "Take me to Gustavo's house," she says.

"I can't do that."

"Yes, you can."

"No."

"I'm not going to knock on his door, I'm not going to break in, I just want to see where he lives."

"You want to see *him*," says Clifford.

"Yes, I want to see him. Why should that surprise you? Gustavo is my husband, and I am going to kill him, and I would like to see him alive just one more time before I see him dead."

"He's not your husband!" Clifford shouts. "He left you! He gave up the right to be your husband when he left you! He's not your husband, he's gone!" *And I'm still here*, he thinks, though he cannot bring himself to remind her.

Madeline laughs, "Fuck, Cliff," and begins polishing her other shoe that is like the other one, cracked and dulled by weather and time and will never shine like new.

Clifford lights a cigarette and goes to the window and inhales deeply, holding the smoke in his lungs until they burn. "You'll change your mind," he says finally.

Madeline does not respond.

Clifford looks at her and insists: "If you see him, you'll change your mind about killing him."

Madeline stands, studies her black patent shoes, frowns. "Just take me to his house."

Of course, he could have refused. He could have said no, insisted on protecting her from knowing, made her see that his refusal was for her own good, was because he loved her, for godsake. But, *esprit d'escalier*, for he is walking along the Boulevard Saint-Michel, toward Beaubourg, Madeline at his side, and it is beginning to rain – a light steady mist that settles on her eyelashes like diamond dust, and on her hair like a net made of diamonds, and on her coat like a glittering impenetrable diamond mail. The diamond in his pocket that she would wear upon becoming his wife feels lighter now than these diamonds of rain that are nearly weightless, less permanent than the rain already vanishing into that state between one form of matter and the next. It is not that he has given up, for he never gives up. It's just that winning has taken on the undesirable shape of a diamond more ordinary than rain.

"Do you still love me?" he asks, voice choked from cold and anguish.

An ungracious pause, then: "What?"

They walk in silence: Clifford summoning the courage to pursue the matter to its unpromising end; Madeline weighing the advantages of truth against lies. But he cannot summon the courage, and she cannot discern between the weight of one thing and another, so the silence persists.

And it is a vast silence: Sunday: The streets especially empty and silent, except:

Somewhere above a shuttered shop, a window is thrown open, through which music escapes: Strauss's *The Emperor's Waltz*. Clifford's and Madeline's footsteps fall into time with the music. And it is no coincidence they both now recall another life lost in another country lost inside winter: the branches of trees clacking in the wind like bones of the hungry dead – hideous accompaniment to the sound of a solitary violin rehearsing *The Emperor's Waltz*, so light, so optimistic by contrast, and Madeline teaching Clifford to waltz while Gustavo rehearsed and watched, laughing when Clifford tumbled backwards over the coffee table, taking Madeline down with him, and Madeline kissing the knot on the back of Clifford's head, and Clifford blushing blood red, and Gustavo sobering, pausing momentarily to watch with displeasure as Madeline kissed Clifford on his blood red cheeks too, first the right then the left – frowning ever so slightly, Gustavo, saying quietly but forcefully, "That is enough, Maddi" before closing his eyes and again lowering his chin onto the fine violin wood, warm and smooth as the inside of a woman's thigh.

It is Clifford's memory of Madeline, and Madeline's memory of Gustavo that causes each to ask himself, herself: *And so what did it mean, after all?*

Here, the street where Gustavo lives. Here, the white stone building that contains his apartment. Here, the apartment window that looks out onto the street. And here, the cafe across the street in which Madeline sits facing the white stone building where Gustavo lives another life in this, another country.

Clifford starts to sit down, but Madeline shakes her head no. He inhales slowly, deeply, loudly, holds his breath and does not let it out until he is outside where he stares up at the tall window behind which Gustavo sleeps, or plays, or fucks – who knows? Clifford lights a cigarette and smokes and stares up at the tall window, repeating silently to himself, like a chant: *Fucking bastard, fucking bastard, fucking bastard...*and smoking and chanting, until finally he flicks the low-burning cigarette into the gutter and walks swiftly, inelegantly away.

The cafe is nearly empty, the one waiter lethargic. It is at least ten minutes before he shuffles over to her table. Even then, she does not notice him – so preoccupied is she with watching the white stone building across the street, expecting the front door to open any moment now and reveal the whole of Gustavo's life lived beyond hers: as rich in music, she presumes, as she is poor in it. She notices now the music inside the cafe – Schubert's *Nachtviolen* – and the waiter who hums along with it, tapping his foot, also staring out at the white stone building.

She says, *"Café, s'il vouz plait."*

The waiter, who is youngish and lanky and scarred by acne, nods and hums *Nachtviolen* and stares across the street a moment longer, then shuffles away.

In memory, even voices are damaged by time, the precise cadence and timbre reduced to their respective descriptors: *hesitant, slightly hoarse.* So that when she recalls the words, "Maddi, I want that you lay with me," they surface as if out of a black twisted river. And is that not the shape of time? And is not every thing drawn into that shape, pulled under by its swift current, so that when the river is dredged for clues to the past, when the past rises again in the present, each memory bears only a slight resemblance to what was once real and vivid and alive.

"Maddi, I want that you lay with me," said Gustavo, voice hesitant, slightly hoarse. He tucked a strand of hair behind her left ear and kissed the ear on its porcelain-thin arch, and whispered, "Lay with me."

She put aside her paint brush full of black ink, not even bothering to rinse the brush or put the lid on the ink pot, for there was nothing she wanted more than to lay with Gustavo, for when she lay with him – scent of autumn leaves in the air, his skin smelling of leaves just fallen – she believed she possessed the soul of the world in her hands, in her mouth, in her cunt and eyes, and they were all turned to gold, and there was nothing nothing nothing more her body or mind or soul required.

And so she lay with Gustavo in the yellow bed in the yellow bedroom, legs locked together, arms entwined, lips brushing against the other's ear. And he said in his hesitant, slightly hoarse voice: *"Te amo, Maddi."* And when she was drifting off to sleep, when it must have appeared to him she had already fallen asleep, she heard the hoarse, hesitant whisper, *"Lo siento."*

And certainly he must have been sorry, already sorry for what he was about to do: Gone the next day, gone so quickly he did not stop even to clean up the mess of black ink spilled on an unfinished drawing of an autumn landscape. Ink spilled on a wet page, spilled wet and bleeding as he rushed out the door on his way to another country, another life.

The waiter brings her coffee and hesitates beside the table as if about to speak. But he does not speak. Instead he again gazes out across the street at the white stone building and sighs. He says something in French, sadly, to the young woman seated at a corner table with a sketchbook propped on her knees, pencil in hand.

She smiles, responds in French, and the waiter sighs again and turns away.

Madeline stares at the young woman without knowing she is staring, until the young woman lifts her pencil from the paper and says, *"Avez-vous envie de voir mes dessins?"*

"I don't speak French," says Madeline,

"Ah!" says the young woman, smiling a pretty smile that transforms her face from something quite ordinary into something nearly beautiful. "You are American?"

"I suppose," says Madeline.

"Pardón?"

"Yes. American."

The young woman nods and smiles. "You want to see?" she asks, holding up the sketchbook with both hands, childlike, eager to exhibit her drawings and practice her English.

Madeline glances across the street at the white stone building that remains unchanged except for the gray light from the Paris sky that has deepened, obliterating all shadows cast upon the cityscape.

She turns to the young woman. "All right."

The young woman grins and pulls her chair alongside Madeline's. She rearranges the cup and saucer and sugar bowl and bud vase upon the table to make room for her sketchbook that she carefully sets in front of Madeline and opens with nervous fingers. On the page: a simple line drawing of the street beyond this cafe window, dressed in autumn, empty as this winter day, silence implied in the clean white planes of paper between the graphite lines. And the lines a remarkable sagacity for an artist so young. Lines that convey the weight of all things succinctly, and the world is somehow made incorruptible.

"Very nice," says Madeline, cloaking her surprise and envy of this young French woman whose talent seems premature, accidental at the very least.

"Ah, thank you!"

Madeline slowly leafs through the sketchbook while the young woman tells about her art studies, her dreams of a future full of art, all the while expectantly watching Madeline's reaction: which is to gaze in awe at each drawing, and to put her hand over her abdomen to calm the tugging there inside, so much like a sexual tugging, a longing to procreate, but a naked longing full of sorrow. She is awed by the creative sensibility that would choose so carefully between the small and the large, balancing them so precisely, so beautifully that what is omitted is never missed. On the contrary, is understood more wholly.

Dear Gustavo: If there is, after all this, a god, then it is a god of minutiae, of all the small things and large things that make up the whole, the weight and weightlessness of life that keep the world spinning, keep us from flying off into empty space, the emptiness of our own desperate souls.

"Your sense of line," Madeline remarks.

"I am sorry?" asks the young artist.

"Your lines," Madeline repeats, tracing a finger over the marks shifting without pause from faint hair-thin tendrils to thick heavy shafts, giving weight and density and life to something that is really nothing more than wood pulp and carbon, "they are...very good." And Madeline is ashamed of the understatement – intentional, jealous – and in her flushing shame bends down to smell the scent of pulp and carbon and a life irrevocably lost.

The young artist smiles in surprise: "Do you love the art?"

"I'm a painter," Madeline nods, then reconsiders: "*Was* a painter," and waves it all away with a flip of her wrist.

"No more the artist?" asks the student, disbelieving or perhaps incapable of believing that the love and consequent pursuit of art might be malleable, impermanent, not a necessity for life.

"No," says Madeline so abruptly that the young artist pulls back her head as if to deflect a blow.

Madeline moves through the sketchbook, one drawing after another wherein the world along this boulevard is rendered lovingly, hopefully: sidewalk cafe in summer, woman piling her hair on top of her head; pavement swept with rain, umbrellas growing like

223

flowers turned away from the sun; a child squatting inside a ring of pigeons.

Madeline turns another page and says, "Oh!" softly, like a moan.

"He is lovely, yes?" says the art student.

Madeline: mute and burning.

"He comes here many times," the art student explains, "but always alone. He takes his coffee here. He speaks to no one, never. His fingers move always on the table, like this," and she taps the fingers of her left hand on the table without a sound. "He sees serious, you know, like this?" and she narrows her eyes, furrows her brow, and stares out the window. "But I think that he sees nothing. No, nothing there in the life of the street. But maybe another life, yes? Another street?" She looks at Madeline and gives a little laugh. "Yes? *Alors*. He is *tres beau?* How do you say – good-looking? But I think also very sad."

Madeline cannot take her eyes from the drawing in which Gustavo's profile is captured with a clarity and objectivity that she herself could have never mastered, obsessive love or rage distorting her vision. She puts a hand to her throat that aches from the grief she cannot release. Puts a hand to her breast that aches from something deeper than sorrow. Looks out the window to see what it is Gustavo sees beyond the tree-lined street, beyond the white stone apartment building and gray sky beyond that. But there is only more gray sky and more, a sense of the world fading to irrelevance.

She clears her throat once, twice, then asks, "Can I buy this?"

"No, I give it to you!"

"You're a student, you must need money. Let me pay you."

The art student shakes her head and carefully tears the drawing from the sketchbook and presents it to Madeline. "He will come to sit again, I am certain! So I will make a drawing the same again."

But he will never come to sit again, Madeline thinks, and the thought fills her with a quick horror, her face and hands and feet going cold, and a quake already swelling inside her breast. And so she excuses herself and hurries to the bathroom and presses her hands flat against the mirror and vomits into the sink.

At L'Hotel Finale a small-time criminal daydreams of notoriety while honing a knife so sharp he can slice the topmost layer of skin from the side of his left thumb, which he does, operating with such deftness that there is no blood, no pain even, only a patch of flesh rendered smooth and pink. He studies the piece of flesh a moment, holding it up to the light to admire its translucency. Then he eats it.

Perhaps because it is no longer in its element — trapped inside a jar from which it stares out at a world that shifts faster than its own shifting skin — the caterpillar's metamorphosis is premature, too soon before spring, a split in the chrysalis already visible. Though Massimo does not yet notice. What he does notice is the silence of a hotel room that only hours before was filled with sighs of pleasure and a name repeated over and over as if repetition would guarantee possession.

He studies his reflection in the mirror and pulls his shoulders straight. "Woman of the gray eyes, I need you."

He can say it now. And wishes to say it. And will say it sooner than later.

Clifford Beale lies on his bed wearing only his boxer shorts and a pair of brown socks. He drinks vodka from a plastic hotel cup and smokes one cigarette after another, pondering the nature of murder and love: how, in another age, he would be a hero: taking revenge on Madeline's broken heart, fighting a duel to the death with pistols – no, swords. Yes, swords: Slashing first Gustavo's shirt sleeve, then his pretty left cheek, then his pretty right, so that after he died – pierced through to the heart – his disfigurement would haunt him throughout the afterlife, an eternal reminder of his adulterous behavior.

When the knock comes at his door, Clifford merely rolls his eyes in its direction, for by now more obvious movement is next to impossible. After the second knock he yells, "Come in!" unconcerned who might appear in his room – unless it is Madeline, of course, fallen out of love with Gustavo and in love with him, Clifford Beale, and ready to beg his forgiveness, and plead her undying love, and get down on her knees and...

Suddenly Massimo is standing at the foot of the bed staring down at Clifford who at first thinks it is Gustavo or the ghost of Gustavo, come to take revenge on his murder. Until Massimo says, "I must to talk with you."

And Clifford asks, "Who the fuck are you?" a fraction of a second before he recognizes Massimo from the train, and so almost immediately adds, "Fucking horny Italian bastard sonofabitch," and tries to raise himself from the bed, but cannot, not without the bed shifting beneath him like a carnival ride. So he lays back down and attempts to rearrange his body into a more dignified posture but sees that he is half naked and brown-socked, and there is no dignity available to him.

"I am come for Madeline Rivera," says Massimo, trying to overcome his own indignity – that of pathetic English – with a straight spine and serious countenance.

"She's not here," says Clifford, lighting another cigarette, though one already burns in the ashtray. "And who the fuck *are* you, anyway?"

Even if Clifford were sober and not slurring his words, Massimo could not understand. But he has prepared for such a disadvantage: He reaches into his pocket and pulls out his police badge and flashes it at Clifford who squints, then squints harder without reaction, so that Massimo is forced to come around to the side of the bed and hold the badge in front of Clifford's face. And it is apparent, then, that Clifford recognizes the badge of an Italian policeman, for the look in his eyes is one of restrained terror and less restrained culpability.

"Madeline Rivera," Massimo repeats with the cold formality of his profession.

Scared half sober, Clifford is already calculating ways to extricate himself from whatever situation he has gotten himself into. He rolls over onto his side to put out his cigarette. He switches from his native tongue to Massimo's: "She's not here."

"So, you speak Italian." Massimo says in Italian, detecting in Clifford's accent what he presumes to be German.

"Yes."

"Good. Tell me: Where is Madeline Rivera?"

"I don't know," Clifford says, which is not exactly a lie since Madeline could be anywhere by now, anywhere: in the cafe, the Louvre, the Seine, Gustavo's apartment, making love to Gustavo... The thought sickens him – or perhaps it is only the vodka and cigarettes. He puts one hand on his belly, the other on his forehead and groans, "I'm sick, I'm sick."

"I don't care," says Massimo. "I want Madeline Rivera."

Clifford laughs bitterly. "Don't we all."

Though it does not conform to the bad-cop role he has taken on, Massimo cannot stop himself from retorting: "She doesn't love you."

"You think I don't know that!" screams Clifford, spit flying, his own voice ricocheting between his temples like a bullet. "You think I don't know she loves Gustavo and not me, or loves nobody and not me, or loves everyone except me, it's all the fucking same!"

Massimo cocks his head sideways. "Who is Gustavo?"

"Her husband!" snaps Clifford.

"Then who are you?" demands Massimo.

Drunk as Clifford is, he is quick to realize the implications of Massimo's ignorance. He sits up, swaying, then eases his legs over the side of the bed. He puts his head in his hands and releases an agonizingly long groan in order to give himself time enough to respond. There is time enough. He responds: "My name is Hans Schweiger. You can check my passport. It's over there, in the back pocket of my jeans."

Massimo checks the passport without turning his back on Clifford Beale, a.k.a. Hans Schweiger, who continues: "I'm just someone she met in Florence. I was on vacation, and she talked me into coming to

Paris with her. She said she had some important business to take care of."

Massimo tosses the passport onto the chair. "What kind of business?"

"I don't know. Something to do with her husband." And because he thinks Massimo now resembles a big fish that has swallowed a big hook, he adds: "I think it concerns his money. Evidently, Gustavo is rich." And the lie feels surprisingly good – *Like a good shit,* thinks Clifford, hiding a grin behind his hands.

Massimo looks up at the cheap fake tapestry on the wall – scene of a bloody ancient war – but sees instead the recent past, a smaller war. But something is not quite right here, thinks Massimo, for he believes he knows Madeline better than anyone, certainly better than Hans Schweiger, probably better than her husband, because he has seen the face behind those empty gray eyes, and it is weeping.

"Where is this Gustavo?" he asks.

"I'm trying to remember if..." Clifford stalls again, rapidly calculating each option and the end result of each option. He surreptitiously checks his watch: a quarter past three. "Oh, yes," he says, "I remember now. He lives in Beaubourg. Here, let me write down the address for you."

"You remember the exact address?" Massimo asks dubiously.

"It's a talent I have," Clifford says. "Remembering numbers."

Just before Massimo leaves he turns to Clifford and asks, "Did you sleep with her?"

Clifford grins. "That's a strange question for a policeman to ask."

And after Massimo is gone Clifford frowns to himself: *That's a very strange question for a policeman to ask.*

It is one thing to contemplate murder from a distance, another to look it in the face, see its pockmarks, its scabs, its sneer.

By the time Madeline walks out of the bathroom, the art student is gone. Only the drawing of Gustavo remains.

The waiter calls to her languidly but earnestly: *"D'argent, ma belle!"* and rubs his thumb and index finger together.

Madeline pulls a handful of francs from her pocket and goes to pay for her coffee. While her back is turned, the bell above the cafe door rings neither fragile nor familiar. Nevertheless, she turns toward it. And for one long deadly silent moment neither she nor Bernard Allande move – both frozen in the shock of the encounter like small animals beneath the stare of a fierce beast.

It is, of course, Bernard Allande who recovers first, breaking into a mirthful grin. He walks toward Madeline, arms outstretched for an embrace.

She stops him with her voice: "The last person I wish to see in my life is you."

Bernard pulls down the corners of his handsome mouth. "I am disappointed, Madeline Rivera. In fact, devastated. I thought we were such good, good friends."

"You're not stupid enough to think that," she says, spinning around to complete her transaction with the waiter.

Bernard takes the opportunity to run his fingers through her hair. She slaps him away, and veers around him toward the exit.

"Why don't you have a coffee with me!" he calls, barely able to contain his glee. "Gustavo will be joining me here shortly."

Madeline halts.

Bernard smirks: "A reunion between the Riveras would be such a pleasure to witness!"

It is a good thing Massimo is uncertain of where he is going, for the yegg has legs much shorter and otherwise would not be able to keep up without running, and he knows the sound of running footsteps is a warning to the pursued because he has pursued many – for luggage, for briefcases, for purses, for wallets – and the few who got away got away because they were warned by running footsteps. So he quickly walks, not runs, behind Massimo – ducking behind trees, pedestrians, trash cans, whatever he can find – each time Massimo stops to ask directions.

"Have you slept with Gustavo?" Madeline asks.

Bernard Allande grins and brushes a strand of blond hair from his forehead. "Slept with, yes. And kissed, fondled, stroked –"

"Fucked?"

"No, he won't allow that." Bernard chuckles. "He seems to think it will make him homosexual. But he'll allow men to suck his cock. And women, of course. And it is a lovely cock, *le zob magnifique, n'est-ce-pas?* So many men and women who wish to suck it. Am I right, Madeline Rivera?"

Madeline shifts uncomfortably in her chair, lights a cigarette, looks out the window at the white stone building, then at her watch.

Bernard grins. "He will be here precisely at four. Gustavo is a man of habits. Most of them bad."

In the lull filled with cafe music – Saint-Saëns *The Swan* – Bernard grows somber. When he speaks it is not so much to Madeline as to the gray-veiled sky above Paris. "Yes. You cannot imagine how bad are Gustavo's habits now. Even I, Bernard Allande, am amazed."

"And jealous?" asks Madeline, for she discerns in his distant gaze something akin to regret.

Bernard Allande snaps his head around and laughs, though his green eyes are filled with an malevolent fire. "Jealous of what? Lovely Madeline, who do you think provides Gustavo with so many opportunities for bad behavior? And not only that," he boasts, "but opportunities for good behavior, also. I have made for your runaway husband many connections here in Paris, important connections in *le monde musique*, and he has taken advantage of them all."

Now it is Madeline's turn to smirk. "And of you, Bernard?"

"Yes, and what of it?" He reaches for her cigarettes without bothering to ask permission. He takes two – slipping one into his breast pocket, lighting the other. He leans back in his chair, gracefully crosses legs, smokes. "We are all whores in one way or another, are we not? Money – well, it is only one form of payment. We use each other for this thing or that thing, to obtain from another person what we cannot attain for ourselves." He shrugs. "Gustavo uses me for my connections in the music world, and I use Gustavo for his

beauty and his charm. The women he does not want
will fuck me just to be near him." He pauses to take a
sip of coffee. "You know, Madeline Rivera, you and I
are not so very different. For example, what was it that
you used Gustavo for? Eh? What thing did he have
that you desired for yourself? Oh, and please do not
say his cock. A woman wanting a cock as her own is so
much the cliché."

Madeline crushes out her cigarette, and looks at the
ashtray when she responds. "I loved Gustavo."

Bernard laughs. "Love! Love is for virgins. Whores
like us – you, me, Gustavo – we overlook the desire to
have love for something more immediate. Music,
money, sex, beauty, the aesthetics of the flesh, yes?
These are immediate. Love is only the name we give
them to make them acceptable to the world, and more
importantly acceptable to ourselves. When you understand this you are free to be a whore without the in-
convenience of guilt. Or to stop being a whore. One or
the other. So what will it be, Madeline Rivera? Whore
or virgin?" He pauses to study her face, then quietly
laughs. "I think maybe you are a moment too late for
the virgin life?"

It is cold. The sky again breaks apart in crystals of
ice, but there is no sunshine now, so the crystals do not
glitter; they are gray and cold.

Cold on the skin, thinks the yegg, rubbing his hands
together, shivering inside his cheap denim jacket. He
leans harder against the trunk of the tree he hides behind, but the bark too is cold and gray, and the chill
enters more deeply into his bones. He reaches into a
pocket and pulls out a slip of paper on which is written
a street address. He looks at the white stone building

two trees away, squints at the number over the door, then looks at Massimo pacing across the street in front of a closed jewelry shop next door to a cafe located directly across from the white stone building. Back and forth and back and forth, Massimo paces: four steps this way four steps that way, pausing only to look across at what is, deduces the yegg, his own apartment building.

"Stupid fuck," mumbles the yegg through chattering teeth. And he considers that there must be some good reason why a man would not enter his own home, some good reason why he would pace back and forth in this bone-chilling cold while inside it must be very warm, by the expensive look of the white stone building, cozy in fact, homey, maybe even a fire burning in the fireplace. And the yegg momentarily drifts off into a warm and cozy room that he cannot enter. Some good reason, he thinks, trembling now. Suspicion, maybe. Suspicion of his own death. And if that is the case, smiles the yegg, checking his watch, then how convenient, for it will be much easier to kill Rivera here on this empty boulevard than in his home, at precisely four o'clock.

"Do you know why I came to Europe?" Madeline asks.

"To find Gustavo," grins Bernard Allande, "and beg him to come back to you."

"No," she says, pausing to light a cigarette, inhale, exhale, glance across at the white stone building, then at Bernard Allande. "I came here to kill him."

Bernard laughs, teeth shining with spit. When Madeline does not react, he laughs harder, bending over as if in pain.

"You don't believe me," she says.

"Oh, but I do!"

"Then why are you laughing?"

"Because it is too perfect, too perfect," says Bernard, still laughing. "The perfect ending to an imperfect relationship. Murder!"

Madeline reaches for another cigarette and notices that her hand is shaking. "Anyway, I've changed my mind, or my heart. I can't tell the difference between one and the other."

"But why change your mind?" Bernard enquires seriously, and he turns to snap his fingers at the waiter. *"Café au lait!"*

"It doesn't matter," says Madeline, again looking at her watch.

Bernard shrugs and glances out the window, not at the white stone building but a little further down the street at a skinny young man dressed in cheap denim who seems peculiarly out of place along this rather elegant block of apartment buildings and expensive shops.

"Tell me," he asks without taking his eyes off the yegg, "how was the crime to be committed?"

"I don't know. Cliff arranged everything."

Bernard snaps his head around. "Cliff? Clifford Beale?"

"Yes."

"That weakling? Ha ha. So perhaps he does have balls after all."

The waiter comes by with Bernard's coffee. He gestures across the boulevard at the white stone building and says something in French, to which Bernard Allande responds in irritation, and the waiter abruptly leaves.

235

"You see?" says Bernard, nodding in the direction of the retreating waiter. "Everyone wants to suck Gustavo's cock."

Everyone but Clifford Beale. Clifford Beale wants to cut off Gustavo's cock and shove it down his throat until he chokes to death. In Clifford's drunken, maddened state the violence of the image starts to give him an erection, and he shudders to loose himself of it.

At the front desk of L'Hotel Finale, he tells one of the Pakistani owners that he wants a pastry with his afternoon tea, a particular pastry sold in a shop along the Boulevard du Montparnasse.

The Pakistani replies, "That is impossible."

Clifford offers him fifty francs.

The Pakistani knows he should be insulted, but money is money. He takes the francs and says he will send his cousin to fetch the pastry.

"He doesn't speak French," Clifford complains. "He'll bring back the wrong pastry, and I will be very unhappy. Why don't you go fetch the pastry and have your brother run the front desk."

"Impossible," repeats the Pakistani. "My brother is away in Rouen for the week."

"Then have your cousin run the desk!" Clifford insists.

The Pakistani considers it a moment, a moment longer...longer...finger tapping his nose, eyes rolled to the ceiling...

Clifford waves another fifty francs in his face.

The Pakistani nods and disappears into the back room, returning with his cousin and an overcoat. Then he is gone.

Clifford gestures to the Pakistani cousin that he would like a cup of tea. The cousin grins, nods, and disappears into the back room. Clifford walks around the desk, opens the center drawer, and takes out the guest registry. He turns to the last page of names, slides a razor blade out of his wallet, and carefully cuts out the page – and the next one to be sure – cuts so carefully it is as if the pages never existed. Then he returns the registry to its drawer and takes a seat in the lobby. He lights a cigarette, then wads up the two pages, places them in the ashtray and sets them on fire. The paper flares and dissolves to black ash, which he crushes with two fingers.

He waits. He pats the thick envelope of money in his pocket for reassurance. He checks his watch. In twenty minutes Gustavo, creature of habit, will walk out of his apartment building and cross the street to have a coffee at the center table in front of the window that looks back at his apartment building – unless Madeline has somehow intervened, ruined everything, unlaid the best laid plans.

The Pakistani cousin returns with a cup of tea. "*Voilà!*" he grins triumphantly.

Clifford grins back, then begins the long laborious gesticulations that earlier got him into Madeline's room. This time, however, it is the yegg's room he wants access to, or more precisely: the yegg's Deutsche marks. Clifford will need them too for the long long trip into another country, another life.

"Cliff's in love with me," Madeline sighs wearily. "He would have done anything I asked."

Bernard Allande tilts his head one way, then the other, watching the dirty denim-clad man behind the tree whose behavior, he has determined, is either the result of madness or calculated transgression. "Clifford Beale may be in love with you, dear Madeline, but I do not think that is his complete reason for killing Gustavo."

"What do you mean?"

He grins at her. *"Cherie,* don't you know?" And he pauses dramatically, satisfied with the dread spreading over Madeline's face. "Gustavo fucked Clifford's girl-friend, Clifford's little angel – what was her name? Kelly, was it not?

"Kelly?"

"You must remember Kelly. The silly one. The one with a brain half the size of my small finger. Clifford brought her to Gustavo's birthday party."

Madeline places the flat of her hand on the table to keep the world from revolving out from under her. "When did Gustavo fuck her, and where?"

Bernard slowly stirs his coffee. "Oh, I think many times. And many, many places. You know Gustavo." He glances up and sneers. "Ah, I forgot. You do not know him at all. In any event, Clifford found out – the stupid girl told him – and he threatened to kill Gustavo. I was back in Paris by then, and Gustavo telephoned me for help. I told him to come to Paris and I would find a way for him to continue to play his music." He grins and winks. "I also suggested he help himself to some of your inheritance."

"Bastard."

"So you see, *ma petite moule,* Gustavo fled. Fled to Paris – via Rome, *merci beaucoup* – in order to save his beautiful ass."

"Who did he take with him? Kelly?"

"He took no one."

"There were two tickets to Rome. He took both."

"Only so you wouldn't follow. But here you are, anyway! Such determination from one so lovely!" And he grabs her face in his hands and tries to plant a kiss on her lips, but she jerks her head away.

Bernard laughs and sits back and lays his palms on his belly as if sated. "Oh, this has been most interesting, most enjoyable. I've been so bored lately, you know? My hands, you see..." And he stares at his swollen fingers as if they are foreign things whose purpose he has not yet determined. He nods slowly. "Yes. They are quite dead to me. And there's only so much fucking one can do to entertain oneself. Ah, well!" He lifts his hands, then presses them hard to his thighs as if to bury them. "So happy to have run into you Madeline. I have few entertainments these days, and I..." He pauses, leans forward. "But you are so pale! What is it?"

"Massimo."

"Massimo?"

She nods at Massimo standing on the curb in front of the cafe. "He must have found out where Gustavo lives."

"And who is Massimo? He looks quite a lot like – "

Madeline looks at Bernard, and it is not without relish that she replies: "My lover."

"*Cherie,*" begins Bernard Allande, voice rising ominously, "for what time exactly did Clifford Beale schedule the murder?"

"I don't know. Sometime tomorrow."

"Are you quite certain *tomorrow*?" he asks as he watches the yegg step out from behind the tree and make haste toward Massimo who is likewise crossing the boulevard now, heading toward the white stone

239

building, wearing on his nearly beautiful face an expression of both determination and dread.

"Yes, Cliff said..." But Madeline does not finish. She is already rising from her chair, elevated by a swelling sense of catastrophe, catastrophe swelling from her weakened knees straight up her spine to her head that pounds out a death march. And the blood in her ears, and the pressure behind her eyes, and the constriction in her throat as if she is being strangled. Which she is: strangled by the thing set in motion, having spun out of control, about to collide with the living.

— seven —

It would happen fast and slow all at once, time relative to participants and viewers alike. What is one moment the presaged future is the next moment the cognizable present is the next moment the selective past.

And it continues on in just such a fashion – black river of time – until no moments remain, thinks Gustavo, tapping a pencil upon a sheet of music silent and incomplete, staring out at the nothing that is the gray-veiled Paris sky.

Under that veil Massimo first glimpses the pale dusty blue of cheap denim, familiar, so near the surface of his memory that he has only to turn his head slightly to the left to recognize the dirty yegg coming toward him: small black eyes delirious with concentrated vio-lence. Second, he glimpses the knife pulled out of a sleeve like a magic trick, hears the music of its *switch!* as the yegg flips open the blade while thrusting it at him – but too early, so that the length of his reach is not quite sufficient: the blade grazing only Massimo's nice woolen coat.

And the yegg grunts, "Uhn!"

And Massimo thinks he hears himself cry out a childish, "Oh!"

And the yegg recoils to strike again.

And it is this second attempt – a horizontal swipe – that reaches its target.

And Massimo stares in displaced wonder at how silently the blade slices through his nice woolen sweater and his belly, how white the exposed layer of fat before the blood comes to obscure it.

At exactly five minutes till four Gustavo, creature of habits bad and good, sets down his pencil and gets up from the desk and walks to the bathroom to wash his hands and study his face in the mirror: shadows beneath the eyes, faint lines around the mouth, the deepening furrows between brows, but still a beautiful face, in fact an astonishing face, one he suspects will be astonishingly beautiful well beyond middle age. And although he lately resents the excessive, almost coercive fawning of women and men, he convinces himself here and now while drying his talented fingers on a clean white towel, that he is grateful for his good looks because they have brought him from an impoverished childhood in Chile, to a position in one of the best chamber orchestras in Europe, and a life of freedom and possibilities. The satisfaction makes him grin, and he runs a finger over his white white teeth.

Creature of habit, but not infallible.

Halfway down the stairs he remembers he is to bring Bernard Allande the name and phone number of a young female cellist, very pretty, who wants private lessons. Thus it is not exactly four o'clock when Gustavo opens the front door of the white stone building, but a moment later – late enough to witness the yegg slicing Massimo's belly, and Massimo gaping at the wound, then grabbing it with both hands and falling to his knees, then toppling over onto his side, legs drawn up like an infant's, nice woolen coat and sweater and trousers turning dark here and there with blood. Late enough to witness the blood spilling, the knife blade wet with blood, the yegg doing a comical sort of dance around Massimo's writhing body in order to calculate where to place the coup de grace. Late enough to forget he is neither infallible nor invincible

and therefore yelling, "Hey, you! Hey!" at the yegg
who spins around to meet the voice and give a startled
gasp, shaking his stupid head violently left to right like
a cartoon character attempting to clear his head,
frowning in confusion at Gustavo's beautiful face, then
frowning at Massimo's – trying to recall from his dull
memory each and every photo of Rivera – then looking
at Gustavo then Massimo then Gustavo until he grows
quite pale, numb even with the horror of his mistake –
already calculating how many Deutsche marks he will
lose if he does not carry out the crime as planned,
wondering now is it worth it, or even possible?

"Merde de merde!" Bernard groans as he watches
Gustavo descend the front steps toward the panicking
yegg. He and Madeline are already on their feet, faces
pressed against the window steaming over from their
tortured breathing. The moment she turns toward the
door he grabs her arm to hold her back while she
struggles to break free, ceasing to struggle only when
Bernard twists her arm hard and screams: "You can do
nothing, nothing! Stay here now and watch the fruits
of your wrath."

And the yegg's panic quickly erodes to rage at the
thought of such injustice, the unjust way things have
played themselves out here in this other country, unjust that God would tease him by sending a man who
looks so much like Rivera but is not Rivera, and unjust
that Rivera and his double would be blessed with so
much beauty when he the yegg is blessed with nothing
but a sharp knife and a suit too cheap to keep out the
cold. Blessed with so much beauty that even the yegg
himself would later confess, after confessing to every-

thing else, that he was mesmerized by the faces of these beautiful men the way one is mesmerized by a great work of art, for example, or a haunting piece of music like, say, his grandfather's favorite aria: Giordano's "La mamma morte."

And so he decides here, within this split second before Gustavo has completely descended the steps, not to run from Rivera but to attack him, specifically attack his mesmerizing face, for therein symbolizes the bulk of his lifelong misery.

Massimo thinks he has died and is gazing up at himself descending the front steps of the white stone building, until he sees the shoes on the feet of the descending figure, quite certain he himself would never wear shoes like those – they are not his style – and thus concluding that the descending man is a stranger interceding in a situation far too dangerous for a civilian. And so he calls out, "No! No!" while trying to motion Gustavo away with his bloody right hand.

But he is too late.

For the knife is raised high in the air and is already making its descent – a vertical stroke intended not so much to kill as disfigure – descending silently, silence encroaching. And, in fact, the world becomes perfectly silent inside the moment that is the absence of time, when Gustavo thoughtlessly raises his left hand to protect his beautiful face, and the knife descends hard, slicing flesh, muscles and tendons down past the knuckles of the index and middle fingers, far down into the palm, at which point the yegg violently twists the blade, once to the left, once to the right, crying, "Uhn!" to the accompaniment of a hand being audibly, irreparably destroyed.

Mi dios mon dieu my god?

And the jealous critic – malicious and obese – rises from his red velvet seat in the back of the rehearsal hall. And grins. And slowly applauds.

Mi dios mon dieu my god!

Gustavo's beautiful face is unharmed.

The crimes are over in a matter of seconds. Precisely: eighteen.

The police have little trouble finding the yegg: No one in all of Paris owns a denim suit so cheap, so dirty.

– eight –

None died. Though some ceased to exist.

The last time anyone saw Clifford Beale he was leaning against a tree trunk near the jewelry shop, smoking a cigarette with one hand, holding a duffle bag with the other, and watching Madeline cross the street toward Massimo. She felt the chill of his eyes upon her and turned to see him open his mouth to let a lungful of smoke roil out. He grinned at her, spit, flicked his cigarette into the gutter, and was gone.

Just before the police arrived, Bernard Allande bent down to stroke Gustavo's beautiful face with his arthritic fingers, and Gustavo reached up with his good hand and punched him in the jaw, and Bernard fell backward onto his ass.

"Ungrateful shit!" screamed Bernard.

Gustavo rolled his eyes up and to the left and said quite clearly, quite calmly: "Maddi, your shoes are bloody." Then he lost consciousness.

Madeline reached a hand halfway toward Gustavo, then let it fall to her side.

Sirens were heard in the distance.

Bernard got to his feet and brushed himself off. He turned to Madeline who was now on her knees on the cold hard pavement, ear held close to Massimo's lips that smiled deliriously and mumbled incomprehensible words – *legato, dolce, leise* – and Bernard said, "Do not worry, Madeline Rivera. Your murderous premeditation will remain a secret with me."

Madeline looked at him suspiciously. "Why, Bernard? Why would you protect me?"

"Protect you?" he laughed, green eyes dancing. "I do not give a fuck what happens to you, Madeline Rivera, whether you live or die or fall somewhere between living and dying. Think of it, *s'il vous plait*, as payment for the pleasure of seeing Gustavo get his – how do you say it? – just desserts?" And he roughly nudged Gustavo's beautiful unconscious head with the toe of his shoe. "The ungrateful shit." And he laughed again, though it was a false laugh full of sickness and pain. He reached in his pocket for the cigarette he had stolen from Madeline's pack and lit it up.

The sirens grew close.

Bernard drew long and deep on the cigarette then bent over Massimo's face. "Congratulations, Madeline, I believe your Massimo is more beautiful than even Gustavo."

Madeline looked at Massimo's face, which was pale and sweating cold, but in his delirium full of a desperate joy, and she had to agree with Bernard. It was not, therefore, without some desperation of her own that she turned to Bernard and pleaded: "Tell me, what's he saying?"

And Bernard listened carefully to Massimo's mumbling, then shrugged. "He says: *The knife of your love.*"

Because Massimo Benevento was an Italian policeman with an excellent service record, from a long line of Italian policemen with excellent service records, the Parisian police never doubted his version of the story: that he and Madeline had come looking for Gustavo to request that he grant Madeline a divorce so that they could marry; that the yegg must have followed them from the train station and may even have been the person who robbed them while they were napping inside their train compartment.

The yegg's story, by contrast, appeared as an elaborate fiction: The police could find no trace of the German man who supposedly had hired the yegg to kill Gustavo for fucking his German wife pregnant. And the yegg did not even know the German man's name. And the yegg's pockets were full of francs not Deutsche marks, nor was there any trace of Deutsche marks in the yegg's room. And L'Hotel Finale's guest registry listed no German man or woman. And the hotel owners denied knowledge of everyone involved, including the yegg, fearing that association with such a heinous crime would cause them to lose L'Hotel Finale's guidebook listings, which had never existed.

And the Pakistani cousin played dumb (which was not difficult for him to do) because he feared his cousins would learn of the bribes he had taken and send him back to Pakistan where he was wanted for the murder of a poor *sarangi* player in Lahore.

And Bernard Allande kept his word, revealing only what he had witnessed with his eyes, not heard with his ears – omitting, of course, the right-hand punch from Gustavo.

And Gustavo who knew nothing, really – at least not at the time – confessed to knowing nothing.

And Madeline Rivera, who was accustomed to interrogations, avoided this one altogether by falling mute and deaf – temporary symptoms brought on, said the Parisian doctors, by severe emotional trauma.

The red wax seal of a German crest remained under the bed of the yegg's hotel room for weeks before a new female maid – quite efficient – found it while cleaning and promptly threw it away.

X. Coda
Bel Canto

It is all airmail, here on this tiny island. The little girl often stands in the front yard, staring up at the sky, waiting for mail to fly down from it, hoping to catch it before the man in the blue uniform catches it, like the big gold butterflies she chases in the garden where her father spends most of his days. She believes the flaps on envelopes are wings that have closed from weariness. After all, her mother tells her, it is a very long way from the continent to this island. A long, long way for mail to travel.

Therefore, today when the man in the blue uniform brings the small brown package, she first opens the flaps to see if there is just enough energy left for it to fly around the yard a while, or maybe around her head. But when she holds the package in her tiny hands and throws it into the air, it merely drops like a dead bird onto the stone walkway.

"Ah, Madelina," her father gently chides, then taps her on the head so that she turns, sees his lips move while his hands sign, silently singing: *What are you doing with that?*

He picks up the package and checks the address label – to Madeline *Rivera* not Madeline *Benevento* –

and his blood goes cold in this warm sunlight. He looks for a return address, but there is only a postmark from New York.

Madelina produces a grunt – her peculiar sort of song – and her tiny hands sign furiously, *Give me! Give me!* stretched as high as they'll go.

"Go inside," he signs, and says gruffly, then recants with a gentle pat on her head, kiss on her cheek.

After she slumps into the house, he unwraps the package and finds inside a new CD: *Reprisal: Requiem in G Minor.* On the back is the composer's photograph: an astonishingly beautiful face, chin resting in a scarred left hand.

Massimo sighs. Stares past the front lawn, past the street and descending hills, past the blue water and thin horizon line. Considers. Decides.

Madeline looks up from the watercolor she has nearly completed. "Come here," she calls to him over the strains of Debussy's *La Mer.* "I want your opinion."

And he goes to her and wraps one arm around her waist and places a big hand on her big pregnant belly and looks over her shoulder at the watercolor of the sea: an abstraction he cannot analyze but can feel in the washes of color that move the way the sea moves when he is floating on it, staring up at the cerulean sky, belly scar shining pink in the sun, sea birds reeling overhead, word on the tip of his tongue: *Libertà!*

He nods: "Very good."

"Very good?" she laughs, cocking her head and squinting up at him. Then she sobers and lays her fingers upon his smooth brown cheek. "What's wrong?"

He looks at her. Looks precisely into gray eyes that are not empty, but full: of contentment, laughter, life. What else precisely? Love? Perhaps.

He considers. Decides.

She studies the CD for a long silent moment, then turns her back to him.

He stares at her narrow shoulders drawn up as if to protect her from some oncoming blow. Eventually they tremble.

On his way out, he turns off the Debussy.

Massimo settles himself on a bench in the garden, alongside perfectly tidy rows of columbine he planted – *How long has it been?* – five years now.

Music bleeds from the doors thrown open onto the terrace, then spills wide over the whole wide garden. *Yes, the whole wide world,* he nods. And beneath the bleeding music – *Such a nice melody, really, sweet and tragic all at once!* – beneath the sweet and tragic music bleeds the not so different music of Madeline weeping.

Il pianto come il dolce spargimento di sangue.

Massimo stares at his hands. How quickly grow the nails, the hair, the lines between the brows! He sighs, "Ah, *sí, sí, sí,*" and raises the middle finger of his left hand to his mouth and bites hard upon the hard nail and tugs at it until it rips away, taking with it a sliver of quick. He winces. Stares at the blood spreading from the tiny wound. Stares a long while, astonished by the blood's color, a red so intense it seems to vibrate. Vibrate with the life still in it, but cooling now, even

here in the warm sun cooling, thus the vibrations of life
fading with the blood's intensity:

¿Que es una vida sin musica?

Massimo glances over his shoulder toward the
music still bleeding but fading too, from a crescendo
down to a solo violin, a soprano keening: *¿Que es...que
es...que es una vida sin musica?* Like a sorrowful woman,
like a designated mourner, like Madeline.

Death.

Yes, life fading even in the warm spring air that
shimmers almost audibly around him as if full of
fluttering tiny-winged birds. And indeed he looks up to
see a hummingbird darting from one columbine to
another, darting swiftly over the quiescent flowers.

Time does not move, he thinks, nodding. *We move.
Death draws near.*

July 5. Another country, another life. Only one of
so many fading lives.

The music bleeds.
Madeline weeps.
The air shimmers.
A hummingbird darts.
Massimo follows it with his black eyes darting too,
and softly hums, humming Verdi's *Requiem aeternum*,
smiling faintly without knowing he is smiling, amazed
by and perhaps grateful for the hummingbird's remarkable shifting silence.

Debra Di Blasi

About the Author

Debra Di Blasi's books include *The Jirí Chronicles & Other Fictions* (FC2/University of Alabama Press, 2007), *Prayers of an Accidental Nature* (Coffee House Press, 1999); and *Drought & Say What You Like (New Directions, 1997)*. Awards include a James C. McCormick Fiction Fellowship from the Christopher Isherwood Foundation, Thorpe Menn Book Award, Diagram Innovative Fiction Award, Cinovation Screenwriting Award, and New Delta Review's Eyster Prize in Fiction, among others. Her fiction has been anthologized and adapted to film, theatre and radio, here and abroad. Essays, reviews, poetry and stories have appeared in *The Iowa Review, New Letters, Notre Dame Review, Pleiades, Exquisite Corpse, Chelsea, Boulevard* and elsewhere. The short film, *Drought*, based on her novella of the same title, was one of only six U.S. films invited to the Universe Elle section of the 2000 Cannes International Film Festival. Her visual and multimedia art has been exhibited in museums and galleries in the U.S. Debra is the inventor of the Diem® Creative Wordplay™ gadget, and president of Jaded Ibis Productions, producing the innovative literature and arts channel BLEED and *The Jirí Chronicles*, a mélange of over 500 fictive audio interviews and music, videos, print, web sites, visual art works, and ironic consumer products. She frequently lectures on 21st Century narratives at colleges and conferences throughout the U.S. and lives in Kansas City, Missouri, with her husband, architect Mark Shapiro.

www.debradiblasi.com

Debra Di Blasi

4075784

Made in the USA
Charleston, SC
24 November 2009